Suzanne's Diary for Nicholas

Suzanne's Diary for Nicholas

James Patterson

**Chivers Press
Bath, England**

This Large Print edition is published by
Chivers Press, England.

Published in 2001 in the U.K. by arrangement with Headline
Book Publishing Ltd.

U.K. Hardcover 0-7540-1707-9 (Windsor Large Print)
U.K. Softcover 0-7540-9106-6 (Paragon Large Print)

The text of this Large Print edition is unabridged.
Other aspects of the book may vary from the original edition.

Set in 16 pt. Plantin by Christina S. Huff.

Printed in the United States on permanent paper.

500624620

*For those who have loved, and lost,
and loved again*

*For Robin Schwarz, whose valuable assistance
and big heart are much appreciated*

*Also, thanks for the help —
Mary, Fern, Barbara, Irene, Maria, Darcy,
Mary Ellen, and Carole Anne*

Most of all, for Suzie and Jack; and for Jane

Katie

Katie Wilkinson sat in warm bathwater in the weird but wonderful old-fashioned porcelain tub in her New York apartment. The apartment exuded "old" and "worn" in ways that practitioners of shabby chic couldn't begin to imagine. Katie's Persian cat, Guinevere, looking like a favorite gray wool sweater, was perched on the sink. Her black Labrador, Merlin, sat in the doorway leading to the bedroom. They watched Katie as if they were afraid for her.

She lowered her head when she finished reading the diary and set the leatherbound book on the wooden stool beside the tub. Her body shivered.

Then she started to sob, and Katie saw that her hands were shaking. She was losing it, and she didn't lose it often. She was a strong person, and always had been. Katie whispered words she'd once heard in her father's church in Asheboro, North Carolina. "Oh, Lord, oh, Lord, are you *anywhere*, my Lord?"

She could never have imagined that this small volume would have such a disturbing effect on her. Of course, it wasn't just the diary that had forced her into this state of confusion and duress.

No, it wasn't just Suzanne's diary for Nicholas.

She visualized Suzanne in her mind. Katie *saw* her at her quaint cottage on Beach Road on Martha's Vineyard.

Then little Nicholas. Twelve months old, with the most brilliant blue eyes.

And finally, Matt.

Nicholas's daddy.

Suzanne's husband.

And Katie's former lover.

What did she think of Matt now? Could she ever forgive him? She wasn't sure. But at least she finally understood some of what had happened. The diary had told her bits and pieces of what she needed to know, as well as deep, painful secrets that maybe she didn't need to know.

Katie slipped down farther into the water, and found herself thinking back to the day she had received the diary — July 19.

Remembering the day started her crying again.

On the morning of the nineteenth, Katie had felt drawn to the Hudson River, and then to the Circle Line, the boat ride around Manhattan Island that she and Matt had first taken as a total goof but had enjoyed so much that they kept coming back.

She boarded the first boat of the day. She was feeling sad, but also angry. Oh, God, she didn't know what she was feeling.

The early boat wasn't too crowded with tourists. She took a seat near the rail of the upper deck and watched New York from the unique vantage point of the brooding waterways surrounding it.

A few people noticed her sitting there alone — especially the men.

Katie usually stood out in a crowd. She was tall — almost six feet, with warm, friendly blue eyes. She had always thought of herself as gawky and felt that people were staring at her for all the wrong reasons. Her friends begged to differ; they said she was close to breathtaking, stunning in her strength. Katie always responded, "Uh-huh, sure, don't I wish." She didn't see herself that way and knew she never would. She was an ordinary, regular person. A North Carolina farm girl at heart.

She often wore her brunette hair in a long braid, and had since she was eight years old. It used to look tomboyish, but now it was supposed to be big-city cool. She guessed she'd finally caught up with the times. The only makeup she ever wore was a little mascara and sometimes lipstick. Today she wore neither. She definitely didn't look breathtaking.

Sitting there on the top deck, she remembered a favorite line from the movie *The African Queen*: "Head up, chin out, hair blowing in the wind, the living picture of the hero-eyne," Bogart had teased Hepburn. It cheered her a bit — a *titch*, as her mother liked to say back home in Asheboro.

She had been crying for hours, and her eyes were puffy. The night before, the man she loved had suddenly and inexplicably ended their relationship. She'd been completely sucker punched. She hadn't seen it coming. It almost didn't seem possible that Matt had left her.

Damn him! How could he? Had he been lying to me all this time — months and months?

12

Of course he had! The bastard. The total creep.

She wanted to think about Matt, about what had happened to separate them, but she wound up thinking of times they'd shared, mostly good times.

Begrudgingly, she had to admit that she had always been able to talk to him freely and easily about anything. She could talk to Matt the way she talked to her women friends. Even her girlfriends, who could be catty and generally had terrible luck with men, liked Matt. *So what happened between us?* That's what she desperately wanted to know.

He *was* thoughtful — at least he *had been.* Her birthday was in June, and he had sent her a single rose every day of what he called "your birthday month." He always seemed to notice whether he'd seen her in a certain blouse or sweater before, her shoes, her moods — the good, the bad, and occasionally the stressed-out ugly.

He liked a lot of the same things Katie did, or so he said. *Ally McBeal, The Practice, Memoirs of a Geisha, The Girl with the Pearl Earring.* Dinner, *then* drinks at the bar at One if by Land, Two if by Sea. Waterloo in the West Village; Coup in the East; Bubby's on Hudson Street. Foreign movies at the Lincoln Plaza Cinema. Vintage black-and-white photos, oil paintings that they found at flea markets. Trips to NoLita (North of Little Italy) and Williamsburg (the new SoHo).

He went to church with her on Sundays, where she taught a Bible class of pre-schoolers. They both treasured Sunday afternoons at her apartment — with Katie reading the *Times* from cover to cover, and Matt revising his poems, which he spread out on her bed and on the bedroom floor and even on the butcher-block kitchen table.

Tracy Chapman or Macy Gray, maybe Sarah Vaughan, would be playing softly in the background. Delicious. Perfect in every way.

He made her feel at peace with herself, completed her circle, did *something* that was good and right. No one else had ever made her feel that way before. Completely, blissfully at peace.

What could beat being in love with Matt?
Nothing that Katie knew of.

One night they had stopped at a little juke bar on Avenue A. They danced, and Matt sang "All Shook Up" in her ear, doing a funny but improbably good Elvis impersonation. Then Matt did an even better Al Green, which completely blew her away.

She had wanted to be with him all the time. *Corny, but true.*

When he was away on Martha's Vineyard, where he lived and worked, they would talk for hours every night on the phone — or send each other funny e-mails. They called it their "long-distance love affair." He had always stopped Katie from actually visiting him on the Vineyard, though. Maybe *that* should have been her early-warning signal?

Somehow, it had worked — for eleven glorious months that seemed to go by in an instant. Katie had expected him to propose soon. She was sure of it. She had even told her mother. But, of course, she had been so wrong that it was pathetic. She felt like a fool — and she hated herself for it.

How could she have been so stupefyingly wrong about him? About everything? It wasn't like her to be this out of touch with her instincts. They were usually *good;* she was *smart;* she didn't do really *dumb things.*

Until now. And, boy, had she made a doozy of a mistake this time.

Katie suddenly realized that she was sobbing and that everyone around her on the deck of the boat was staring at her.

"I'm sorry," she said, and motioned for them to please look away. She blushed. She was embarrassed and felt like such an idiot. "I'm okay."

But she wasn't okay.

Katie had never been so hurt in her life. Nothing came close to this. She had lost the only man she had ever loved; God, how she loved Matt.

Katie couldn't bear to go in to work that day. She couldn't face the people at her office. Or even strangers on a city bus. She'd gotten enough curious looks on the boat to last a lifetime.

When she got back to her apartment after her trip on the Circle Line, a package was propped up against the front door.

She thought it was a manuscript from the office. She cursed work under her breath. Couldn't they leave her alone for a single day? She was entitled to a personal day now and then. God, she worked so hard for them. They knew how passionate she was about her books. They knew how much Katie cared.

She was a senior editor at a highly thought of, collegial, very pleasant New York publishing house that specialized in literary novels and poetry. She loved her job. It was where she had met Matt. She had enthusiastically bought his first volume of poetry

17

from a small literary agency in Boston about a year before.

The two of them hit it off right away, *really* hit it off. Just weeks later they had fallen in love — or so she had believed with her heart, soul, body, mind, woman's intuition.

How could she have been so wrong? What had happened? Why?

As she reached down for the package, she recognized the handwriting. *It was Matt's.* There was no doubt about it.

She wanted to hurl the package away with all the power and strength in her body, and nearly dropped it.

She didn't. Too much self-control — that was her problem. *One* of her problems. Katie stared at the package for some time. Finally, she took a deep breath and tore away the brown paper wrapping.

What she found inside was a small antique-looking diary. Katie frowned. She didn't understand. Then she felt her stomach begin to knot.

Suzanne's Diary for Nicholas was handwritten on its front cover — handwritten, but it wasn't Matt's handwriting.

Suzanne's?

Suddenly Katie's head was reeling and she could barely catch a breath. She couldn't think straight, either. Matt had always been closemouthed and secretive about his past. One of the things she had found out was that his wife's name was Suzanne. That much had slipped out one night after they had drunk two bottles of wine. But then Matt hadn't wanted to talk about Suzanne.

The only arguments they'd ever had were over the silence about his past. Katie had insisted on knowing more, which only made Matt quieter and more mysterious. It was so unlike him. After they actually had a fight about it, he'd told her that he wasn't married to Suzanne anymore; he swore it, but that was all he was going to say on the subject.

Who was Nicholas? And why had Matt sent her this diary? Why now? She was completely puzzled, and more than a little upset.

Katie's fingers were trembling as she opened the diary to its first page. A note from Matt was affixed. Her eyes began to well up, and she angrily wiped the tears away. She read what he'd written.

Dear Katie,

No words or actions could begin to tell you what I'm feeling now. I'm so sorry about what I allowed to happen between us. It was all my fault, of course. I take all the blame.

You are perfect, wonderful, beautiful. It's not you. It's me.

Maybe this diary will explain things better than I ever could. If you have the heart, read it.

It's about my wife and son, and me.

I will warn you, though, there will be parts that may be hard for you to read.

I never expected to fall in love with you, but I did.

Matt

Katie turned the page.

The Diary

Dear Nicholas, my little prince —

There were years and years when I wondered if I would ever be a mother.

During this time, I had a recurring daydream that it would be so wonderful and wise to make a videotape every year for my children and tell them who I was, what I thought about, how much I loved them, what I worried about, the things that thrilled me, made me laugh or cry, made me think in new ways. And, of course, all my most personal secrets.

I would have treasured such videotapes if my mother and father had recorded them each year, to tell me who they were, what they felt about me and the world.

As it turned out, I don't know who they are, and that's a little sad. No, it's a lot sad.

So, I am going to make a videotape for you every year — but there's something else I want to do for you, sweet boy.

23

I want to keep a diary, *this* diary, and I promise to be faithful about writing in it.

As I write this very first entry, you are two weeks old. But I want to start by telling you about some things that happened before you were born. I want to start *before* the beginning, so to speak.

This is for your eyes only, Nick.

This is what happened to Nicholas, Suzanne, and Matt.

Let me start the story on a warm and fragrant spring evening in Boston. I was working at Massachusetts General Hospital at the time. I had been a physician for eight years. There were moments that I absolutely loved, cherished: seeing patients get well, and even being with some when it was clear they wouldn't recover. Then there were the bureaucracy and the hopeless inadequacy of our country's current healthcare program. There were my own inadequacies as well.

I had just come off a twenty-four-hour rotation and I was tired beyond anything you can imagine. I was out walking my trusted and faithful golden retriever, Gustavus, a.k.a. Gus.

I suppose I should give you a little snapshot of myself back then. I had long blond hair, stood about five foot five, not exactly beautiful but nice enough to look at, a friendly smile most of the time, for most of the human race. Not *too* caught up in appearances.

It was a late Friday afternoon, and I remember that the weather was so nice, the air was sweet and as clear as crystal. It was the kind of day that I live for.

I can see it all as if it just happened.

Gus had sprinted off to harass and chase a poor, defenseless city duck that had wandered away from the safety of the pond. We were in the Boston Public Garden, by the swan boats. This was our usual walk, especially if Michael, my boyfriend, was working, as he was that night.

Gus had broken from his lead, and I ran after him. He is a gifted retriever, who lives to retrieve anything: balls, Frisbees, paper wrappers, soap bubbles, reflections on the windows of my apartment.

As I ran after Gus, I was suddenly struck by the worst pain I have ever felt in my life. *Jesus, what is this?*

It was so intense that I fell to my hands and knees.

Then it got worse. Razor-sharp knives were shooting up and down my arm, across my back, and into my jaw. I gasped. I couldn't catch my breath. I couldn't focus on anything in the Public Garden. Everything was a blur. I couldn't actually be sure of what was happening to me, but something told me *heart*.

What was wrong with me?

I wanted to cry out for help, but even a few words were beyond me. The tree-laden Garden was spinning like a whirligig. Concerned people began crowding around, then hovering over me.

Gus had come skulking back. I heard him barking over my head. Then he was licking my cheek, but I barely felt his tongue.

I was flat on my back, holding my chest.

Heart? My God, I am only thirty-five years old.

"Get an ambulance," someone cried. "She's in trouble. I think she's dying."

I am not! I wanted to shout. *I can't be dying.*

My breathing was becoming shallower and I was fading to black, to nothingness. *Oh, God,* I thought. *Stay alive, breathe, keep conscious, Suzanne.*

That's when I remember reaching out for a stone that was near me in the dirt. *Hang on to this stone,* I thought, *hang on tight.* I believed it was the only thing that would keep me attached to the earth at that scary moment. I wanted to call out for Michael, but I knew it wouldn't help.

Suddenly I realized what was happening to me. I must have passed out for several minutes. When I came to, I was being lifted into an ambulance. Tears streamed down my face. My body was soaked with sweat.

The EMT woman kept saying, "You're gonna be fine. You're all right, ma'am." But I knew I wasn't.

I looked at her with whatever strength I could muster and whispered, "Don't let me die."

All the while I was holding the small stone tightly in my hand. The last thing I recall is an oxygen mask being slipped over my face, a deathly weakness spreading through my body, and the stone finally dropping from my hand.

So, Nicky,

I was only thirty-five when I had the heart attack in Boston. The following day I had a coronary bypass at Mass. General. It put me out of action, out of circulation for almost two months, and it was during my recuperation that I had time to think, really think, maybe for the first time in my life.

I thoroughly, painfully examined my life in Boston, just how hectic it had become, with rounds, research, overtime, overwork, and double shifts. I thought about how I'd been feeling just before this awful thing happened. I also dealt with my own denial. My grandmother had died of heart failure. My family had a history of heart disease. And still I hadn't been as careful as I should have been.

It was while I was recuperating that a doctor friend told me the story of the five balls. You should never forget this one,

Nicky. This is terribly important.

It goes like this.

Imagine life is a game in which you are juggling five balls. The balls are called work, family, health, friends, and integrity. And you're keeping all of them in the air. But one day you finally come to understand that work is a rubber ball. If you drop it, it will bounce back. The other four balls — family, health, friends, integrity — are made of glass. If you drop one of these, it will be irrevocably scuffed, nicked, perhaps even shattered. And once you truly understand the lesson of the five balls, you will have the beginnings of balance in your life.

Nicky, *I finally understood.*

Nick —

As you can probably tell, this is all pre-Daddy, pre-Matt.

Let me tell you about Dr. Michael Bernstein.

I met Michael in 1996 at the wedding reception for John Kennedy and Carolyn Bessette on Cumberland Island, Georgia. I must admit that both of us had led pretty charmed lives up until then. My parents had died when I was two, but I was fortunate enough to have been raised with great love and patience by my grandparents in Cornwall, New York. I went to Lawrenceville Academy in New Jersey, then Duke, and finally Harvard Medical School.

I felt incredibly lucky to be at each of the three schools, and I couldn't have gotten a better education — except that nowhere did I learn the lesson of the five balls.

Michael also went to Harvard Medical

31

School, but he had graduated four years before I got there. We didn't meet until the Kennedy wedding. I was a guest of Carolyn's; Michael was a guest of John's. The wedding itself was magical, full of hope and promise. Maybe that was part of what drew Michael and me together.

What kept us together for the next four years was a little more complicated. Part of it was pure physical attraction, and at some point I want to talk to you about that — but not now. Michael was — *is* — tall and dashing, with a radiant smile. We had a lot of mutual interests. I loved his stories, always so droll, laconic, biting; I loved to listen to him play the piano and sing anything from Sinatra to Sting. Also, we were both workaholics — me at Mass. General, Michael at Children's Hospital in Boston.

But none of these things are what love is really about, Nicholas. Trust me on that.

About four weeks after my heart attack, I woke up one morning at eight o'clock. The apartment where we lived was quiet, and I luxuriated in the peacefulness for a few moments. It seemed to have a healing quality. Finally I got up and went to the kitchen to make myself breakfast before I went off to rehab.

I jumped back when I heard a noise, the

scratch of a chair leg against the floor. Nervously, I went to see who was out there.

It was Michael. I was surprised to see him still home, as he was almost always out of the house by seven. He was sitting at the small pine table in the breakfast nook.

"You almost gave me a heart attack," I said, making what I thought was a pretty decent joke.

Michael didn't laugh. He patted the chair next to him at the table.

Then, with the calmness and self-reverence I was used to from him, he told me the three main reasons why he was leaving me: he said he couldn't talk or relate to me the way he could with his male friends; he didn't think that I could have a baby now, because of my heart attack; he had fallen for someone else already.

I ran out of the kitchen, and then out of the house. That morning the pain I felt was even worse than the heart attack. Nothing was right with my life; I had gotten it all wrong so far. *Everything!!!*

I did love being a doctor, but I was trying to do it in a large, somewhat bureaucratic, big-city hospital, which just wasn't right for me.

I was working so hard — because there was nothing else of value in my life. I earned about

33

$120,000 a year, but I was spending it on dinners in town, getaway weekends, clothes that I didn't need or even like that much.

I had wanted children all my life, yet here I was without a significant other, without a child, without a plan, and no prospects to change any of it.

Here's what I did, little boy.

I began to *live* the lesson of the five balls.

I left my job at Mass. General. I left Boston. I left my murderous schedule and commitments behind. I moved to the one place in the world where I had always been happy. I went there, truly, to mend a broken heart.

I was turning endlessly around and around like a hamster on a wheel in a tiny cage. My life was stretched to the limit, and something was bound to give. Unfortunately, it had been my heart.

This wasn't a small change, Nicky; I had decided to change everything.

Nicky,

I arrived on the island of Martha's Vineyard like an awkward tourist, lugging the baggage of my past, not knowing what to do with it yet. I would spend the first couple of months filling cupboards with wholesome, farm-fresh foods, throwing out old magazines that had followed me to my new home, and I would also settle into a new job.

From the time I was five until I was seventeen, I had spent summers with my grandparents on Martha's Vineyard. My grandfather was an architect, as my father had been as well, and he could work from his home. My grandmother Isabelle was a homemaker, and she was gifted at making our living space the most comfortable and loving place I could begin to imagine.

I loved being back on the Vineyard, loved everything about it. Gus and I often went to the beach in the early evening, and we sat out there until the light of day was gone. We played ball, or sometimes with a Frisbee for the first hour or so. Then we huddled together on a blanket until the sun went down.

I had negotiated for the practice of a general practitioner who was moving to Illinois. We were switching lives in some ways. He was going to Chicago just when I was exiting city life. My office was one of five doctors' offices in a white clapboard house in Vineyard Haven. The house was more than a hundred years old and had four beautiful antique rockers on the front porch. I even had a rocker at the desk where I worked.

Country doctor resonated with a wonderful sound for me, like recess bells of an old country school. I was inspired to hang out a shingle that said as much: SUZANNE BEDFORD — COUNTRY DOCTOR — IN.

I began to see a few patients in my second month on Martha's Vineyard.

Emily Howe, seventy, part-time librarian, honored member of the Daughters of the American Revolution, hard, steadfast, and against everything that had occurred since about 1900. Diagnosis: bronchitis; Prognosis: good.

Dorris Lathem, ninety-three, had already outlived three husbands, eleven dogs, and a house fire. Healthy as a horse. Diagnosis:

old gal; Prognosis: will live forever.

Earl Chapman, Presbyterian minister. General Outlook — always his own. Diagnosis: acute diarrhea; Prognosis: possible recurrence of what the Lord might call getting even.

My first patient list read like a who's who of a William Carlos Williams poem. I imagined Dr. Williams walking the streets of the Vineyard on his appointed rounds, an icy wind blowing from the distant hills, milk frozen on every landing, the famous wheelbarrow soldered into the winter mud. There he'd be, making a late-afternoon call on the boy who fell off his sled and broke an arm along with his pride.

This was for me. I was experiencing a fantasy that was a million miles away when I lived in Boston.

But, in fact, it was just down Route 3 and across the water.

I felt I had come home.

Nicholas,

I had no idea that the love of my life was here — just waiting for me. If I had, I would have run straight into Daddy's arms. In a heartbeat.

When I first arrived on Martha's Vineyard, I was unsure about everything, but especially where to settle. I drove around looking for something that said "home," "you'll be okay here," "look no further."

There are so many parts of our island that are beautiful, and even though I knew it in some ways, it sang out differently to me this time.

Everything was different because *I* felt different. Up Island was always special to me, because this is where I had spent so many glorious summers. It lay like a child's picture book of farms and fences, dirt roads, and cliffs. Down Island was a whirl of widow's walks, gazebos, lighthouses, and harbors.

It was a turn-of-the-century boathouse

that finally stole my heart. And still does. This truly was home.

It needed to be fixed up, but it was winterized, and I loved it at first sight, first smell, first touch. Old beams — which had once supported stored boats — crisscrossed the ceiling. Upstairs I eventually put in corner portholes to let the sun come in in hoops of light. The walls *had* to be painted robin's-egg blue because the whole downstairs opened to a view of the sea. Big barnlike doors slid port and starboard to bring everything that was once outside, *inside*.

Can you imagine, Nicky, living practically right on the beach, like that? Every part of me, body and soul, knew I'd made the right decision. Even my sensible side was in agreement. I now lived between Vineyard Haven and Oak Bluffs. Sometimes I'd be working out of my home or making house calls, but the rest of the time I'd be at Martha's Vineyard Hospital or the Vineyard Walk-In Medical Center in Vineyard Haven. I was also doing some cardiology rehab at the Medical Center.

I was alone, except for Gus, living a solitary life, but I was content for the most part.

Maybe it was because I had no idea what I was missing at the time: *your daddy and you.*

Nicholas,

I was driving home from the hospital when I heard a funny noise. What's that? *Shhhhh . . . bump shhhh . . . bump shhhh . . . bump.*

I had to pull over onto the shoulder of the road. I got out of my Jeep to take a look.

Shitfire and save matches. The right wheel was as flat as a pancake. I could have, and I would have, changed the tire if I hadn't taken out the spare in order to make room for all my other stuff when I was moving.

I called the gas station from my cell phone, mad at myself for having to call a garage. A guy answered and condescended to me a little; *another* guy would come to fix the flat. It made me feel like "such a girl," and I hated that. I knew how to change a tire perfectly well. I pride myself on self-sufficiency and independence. And good old-fashioned stubbornness.

I was standing against the passenger-side

door, pretending to admire the beautiful landscape and making it seem to passing cars that I had pulled over for that reason, when a car pulled up right in back of mine.

Clearly it wasn't from the gas station.

Not unless they'd sent a forest green Jaguar convertible.

"You need some help?" a man asked. He was already walking slowly toward my car, and honestly, I couldn't take my eyes off him.

"No, thanks . . . I called the Shell station in town. They'll be here soon. Thanks, anyway."

There was something familiar about this guy. I wondered if I had met him in one of the stores around the island. Or maybe at the hospital.

But he was tall and good-looking, and I thought that I'd have remembered him. He had a nice, easy smile and he was kind of laid-back.

"I can change the tire," he offered, and somehow managed *not* to be condescending when he said it. "I know I drive a fancy car, but I'm not really a fancy person."

"Thanks, but I took my spare out to make room for more important things like my stereo and my antique candlestick collection."

He laughed . . . and he was *so familiar.*

41

Who was he? Where did I know him from?

"I'm flattered, though," I continued. "A man in a shiny convertible willing to change a tire."

He laughed again — a nice laugh. *So familiar.*

"Hey, I'm vast. . . . I contain multitudes."

"Walt Whitman!" I said — and then I remembered who this was. "You used to say that *all the time.* You quoted Walt Whitman. *Matt?*"

"Suzanne Bedford!" he said. "I was almost sure it was you."

He was so surprised — bumping into me like this after such a long time. It must have been almost twenty years.

Matt Wolfe was even handsomer than I remembered him. At thirty-seven, he had grown up very nicely. He was slender, with closely cropped brown hair and an endearing smile. He looked in great shape. We talked on the side of the road. He had become a lawyer for the Environmental Protection Agency as well as a fine-arts dealer. I had to laugh when he told me that. Matt used to joke that he would never become an *entremanure,* as he called businesspeople back then.

He wasn't surprised to learn that I was a doctor. What surprised Matt was that I wasn't with someone, that I had come back to Martha's Vineyard *alone*.

We continued to catch up on each other's life. He was funny, easy to talk to. When I had dated Matt, he was eighteen, I was sixteen. That was the last year my grandparents had rented for the summer on the Vineyard — but obviously, I never forgot the island or its many treasures. I'd been having dreams about the ocean and the beaches on the Vineyard ever since I could remember.

I think we were both a little disappointed to see the bright yellow Shell tow truck pull in behind us. I know that I was. Just before I turned to go, Matt mumbled a few words about how nice this was — my flat tire. Then he asked me what I was doing Saturday night.

I think I blushed. I know I did. "You mean a date?"

"Yes, Suzanne, a date. Now that I've seen you again, I'd like to see you *again*."

I told Matt I would love to see him on Saturday. My heart was pounding a little, and I took that to be a very good sign.

Nick,

Who the heck was sitting on my porch? As I drove up late that same afternoon, I couldn't really tell.

It couldn't be the electric guy, or the phone guy, or the cable guy — I'd seen all of them the day before.

Nope, it was the painting guy, the one who was going to help me with everything around the cottage that needed a ladder or an outlet or a finish.

We walked around the cottage as I pointed out several of the problems I'd inherited: windows that wouldn't close, floors that buckled at the door, a leak in the bathroom, a broken pump, a cracked gutter, and a whole cottage that needed scraping and painting.

What this house had in cute, it lacked in practical.

But this guy was great, took notes, asked

pertinent questions, and told me he could fix everything by the millennium. The next millennium. We struck a deal on the spot (which gave me the distinct feeling I'd made out pretty good).

Suddenly life was looking a lot better to me. I had a new practice that I loved, I had a housepainter with a good reputation, and I had a hot date with Matt.

When I was finally alone in my little cottage by the sea, I threw up both arms and shouted hooray.

Then I said, "Matt Wolfe. Hmmm. Imagine that. How terrific. How very cool."

Nick,

Just about everybody has an occasional fantasy about somebody they really liked in high school, or maybe even grade school, coming back into their life. For me, that person was Matt.

Who knows, maybe he was a small part of what drew me back to Martha's Vineyard. Probably not, but who can tell about these things?

Nevertheless, I was nearly an hour late for our date on Saturday night. I had to get a patient admitted, run home and feed Gustavus, get pretty, and find my beeper all before I left. Plus — I must confess — I can be a bit disorganized at times. My grandfather used to say, "Suzie, you have a lot *in* your mind."

When I entered Lola's, which is a neat spot on the beach between Vineyard Haven and Oak Bluffs, Matt was waiting with a bottle of pinot noir. He looked relaxed, and I liked that.

Also handsome. I liked that just fine, too.

"Matt, I'm so, so sorry," I said. "This is one of the negatives about dating a doctor."

He laughed. "After twenty years . . . what's twenty minutes? Or fifty? And besides, you look beautiful, Suzanne. You're worth the wait."

I was flattered, and a little embarrassed. It had been a while since someone had paid me a compliment, even as a joke. But I liked it. And I eased smoothly into the evening like someone slipping into satin sheets.

"So, you're back on the Vineyard for good?" Matt asked after I told him some, but not all, of the events that had led up to my decision. I didn't tell him about the heart attack. I would, but not yet.

"I love it here. Always have. I feel like I've come home," I said. "Yes, I'm back here for good."

"How are your grandparents?" he asked. "I remember them both."

"My grandfather's still alive, and he's doing great. Grandmother died six years ago. Her heart."

Matt and I talked and talked — about work, summers on the Vineyard, college, our twenties, thirties, successes, disappointments. He had spent his twenties living all over the world: Positano, Madrid, London,

New York. He'd gotten into New York University Law School when he was twenty-eight, moved back to the Vineyard two years ago. Loved it. It felt so good to talk to him again; it was such a nice trip down memory lane.

After dinner Matt followed me home in his Jag. He was just being thoughtful. We both got out in the driveway and talked some more under a beautiful full moon. I was really enjoying myself.

He started to laugh. "Remember our first date?"

Actually, I did. There had been a wicked thunderstorm and it knocked out the electricity in my house. I had to get dressed in the dark. By mistake, I picked up a can of Lysol instead of hair spray. I smelled of disinfectant all night.

Matt grimaced and asked, "Do you remember the first time I got my nerve up to kiss you? Probably not. I was scared."

That surprised me a little. "I couldn't tell. As I remember it, you were always pretty confident."

"My *lips* were shaking, my teeth hitting together. I had the biggest crush on you. I wasn't the only one."

I laughed. This was silly, but it sure was fun. In a way, seeing Matt again was a fantasy come true. "I don't believe any of this, but I love hearing it."

"Suzanne, could I kiss you?" he asked in a gentle voice.

Now *I* was shaking a little. I was out of practice at this. "That would be okay. That would be good, actually."

Matt leaned over and, in the sweetest way, kissed me. A kiss, just one. But it was really something after all these years.

Dear Nicky,

Bizarre! That's the only word I can use to describe life sometimes. Just freaking bizarre.

Remember the housepainter I told you about? Well, he was over here the morning after my date with Matt, giving the joint a face-lift. I know this because he left me a bouquet of the most beautiful wildflowers.

There they were — pinks, reds, yellows, blues, and purples, sitting pretty in a mason jar by the front door.

Very sweet, very nice, and unexpectedly touching.

At first I thought they were from Matt, but damn it, they weren't.

There was also a note. *Dear Suzanne, The lights are still out in your kitchen, but I hope these will brighten your day some. Maybe we can get together sometime and do whatever you want to do, whenever you want to, wherever you want to.* He signed himself

Picasso — more readily known as your house-painter.

I was blown away. Until the night before, I hadn't had a date since I left Boston; I hadn't wanted to date since Michael Bernstein left me.

Anyway, I heard the painter-maintenance man hammering something somewhere, and I went outside. There he was, perched like a gull on the steep slanted roof.

"Picasso," I yelled, "thank you so much for the beautiful flowers. What a nice present. A nice thought."

"Oh, you're welcome. They just reminded me of you, and I couldn't resist."

"Well, you guessed right; they're all my favorites."

"What do you think, Suzanne? Maybe we could grab a bite sometime, go for a ride, catch a movie, play Scrabble. Did I leave anything out?"

I smiled in spite of myself.

"It's kind of a crazy time for me right now, with patients and all. I just have to make that a priority for the time being. But it was really nice of you to ask."

He took the rejection in stride. He smiled down at me. But then he ran his hand through his hair and said, "I understand. Of course you realize if you don't go out with me just once, I'll have no choice but to raise your rates."

I called back to him, "No, I didn't know that."

"Yeah. It's absolutely despicable, a totally unfair business practice. But what can you do? It's the way of the world."

I laughed, and told him I'd take that under serious consideration. "Hey, by the way, what do I owe you for the extra work you've already done over the garage?" I asked.

"That? That's nothing . . . nothing at all. No charge."

I shrugged, smiled, waved. What he'd said was nice to hear — maybe because it *wasn't* the way of the world.

"Hey, thanks, Picasso."

"Hey, no problem, Suzanne."

And he resumed his task of putting a roof over my head.

Dear Nicholas,

I am watching over you as I write this, and you are absolutely gorgeous.

Sometimes I look at you and just can't believe you're mine. You have your father's chin, but you definitely have my smile.

There's a little toy that hangs over your crib and when you pull on it, it plays "Whistle a Happy Tune." This makes you laugh immediately. I think Daddy and I love to hear that song as much as you do.

Sometimes at night, if I'm driving home late or taking a walk, I'll hear that little melody in my head, and I'll feel such longing for you.

Right now, I just want to pick you up out of your sleep and hold you as close as I can.

The other thing that always makes you laugh is "One Potato, Two Potato." I don't know why. Maybe it's the sound of it, the silly lyrical bounce of the words. Maybe it's the part of you that's Irish. All I know is, the word *potato* can send you into fits and wiggles of happiness.

Sometimes I can't imagine your being any other age than the one you are this second. But I think all mothers tend to hold their children frozen in time, or maybe pressed like flowers, forever perfect, forever eternal. Sometimes when I rock you, I feel as if I were holding a little bit of heaven in my arms. I have a sense that there are protective angels all around you, all around us.

I believe in angels now. Just looking at you, sweet baby boy, I would have to.

I'm thinking about how much I loved you when you were in mommy's tummy. I loved you *the moment we met.* Seeing you for the first time, you looked right at Daddy and me. The look in your eyes said "Hey I'm here, hi!"

You were incredibly alert, checking everything out. Finally, Daddy and I could see you after nine months of imagining what you would be like. I took your head and pulled it gently to my chest. You were six pounds three ounces of sheer happiness.

After I held you, Daddy held you next. He couldn't believe how a baby, just minutes old, could be looking back at him.

Matt's little boy.

Our beautiful little Nicholas.

54

Katie

Matt's little boy.
Our beautiful little Nicholas.

Katie Wilkinson put down the diary, sighed, and took a deep breath. Her throat felt raw and sore. She ran her fingers through Guinevere's soft gray fur, and the cat purred gently. She blew her nose into a tissue. She hadn't been ready for this. She definitely hadn't been ready for Suzanne.

Or Nicholas.

And especially not Nicholas, Suzanne, and Matt.

"This is so crazy and so bad, Guinny," she said to the cat. "I've gotten myself into such a mess. God, what a disaster."

Katie got up and wandered around her apartment. She had always been so proud of it. She had done much of the work herself, and liked nothing better than to throw on a T-shirt, cutoffs, and work boots, then build and hang her own cabinets and bookcases. Her place was filled with authentic antique pine, old hooked rugs, small water-colors like the one of the Pisgah Bridge, just south of Asheboro.

Her grandmother's jelly cabinet was in her study, and the interior planks still held the aroma of homemade molasses and jellies. Several vellum-paged, hand-sewn board books were displayed in the jelly cabinet. Katie had made them herself. She'd learned bookbinding at the Penland School of Crafts in North Carolina.

There was a phrase she loved, and also lived by — Hands to work, hearts to God.

She had so many questions right now, but no one to answer them. No, that wasn't completely true, was it? She had the diary.

Suzanne.

She liked her. Damn it, she liked Suzanne. She hadn't wanted to — but there it was. Under different circumstances they might have been friends. She *had* friends like Suzanne in New York and back home in North Carolina. Laurie, Robin, Susan, Gilda, Lynn — lots of really good friends.

Suzanne had been gutsy and brave to get out of Boston and move to Martha's Vineyard. She had chased her dream to be the kind of doctor, the kind of woman, she needed to be. She had learned from her near-fatal heart attack: she'd learned to treasure

58

every moment as a *gift*.

And what about Matt? What had Katie meant to him? Was she just another woman in a doomed affair? God, she felt as if she should be wearing the Scarlet Letter. Suddenly she was ashamed. Her father used to ask her a question all the time when she was growing up: "Are you right with God, Katie?" She wasn't sure now. She didn't know if she was right with anyone. She had never felt that way before, and she didn't like it.

"Jerk," she whispered. "You creep. Not *you*, Guinevere. I'm talking about Matt! Damn him!"

Why didn't he just tell her the truth? Had he been cheating on his perfect wife? Why hadn't he wanted to talk about Suzanne? Or Nicholas?

How could she have allowed Matt to seal off his past from her? She hadn't pushed as much as she could have. Why? Because it wasn't her style to be pushy. Because she didn't like being pushed herself. She certainly didn't like confrontations.

But the most compelling reason had been the look in Matt's eyes whenever they started to talk about his past. There was such sadness — but also intimations of anger. And Matt had *sworn* to her that he

59

was no longer married.

Katie kept remembering the horrible night Matt left her. She was still trying to make sense of it. Had she been a fool to trust *someone she thought she loved?*

On the night of July 18, she had prepared a special dinner. She was a good cook, though she seldom had the time to do this kind of elaborate affair. She'd set the wrought-iron table on her small terrace with her beautiful Royal Crown Derby china and her grandmother's silver. She'd bought a dozen roses, a mixture of red and white. She had Toni Braxton, Anita Baker, Whitney, and Eric Clapton on the CD player.

When Matt arrived, she had the best, the most wonderful surprise waiting for him. It was really great: the first copy of the book of poems he'd written, which she had edited at the publishing house where she worked. It had been a labor of love. She also gave him the news that the printing was 11,500 copies — very large for a collection of poems. "You're on your way. Don't forget your friends when you get to the top," she'd said.

Less than an hour later, Katie found herself in tears, shaking all over, and feeling as if she were living a horrible nightmare that couldn't possibly be real. Matt had barely come in the door when she knew something was wrong. She could see it in his eyes, hear it in the tone of his voice. Matt had finally told her, "Katie, I have to break this off. I can't see you again. I won't be coming to New York anymore. I know how awful that sounds, how unexpected. I'm sorry. I had to tell you in person. That's why I came here tonight."

No, he had no idea how awful it sounded, or was. Her heart was broken. It *still* was broken. She had trusted him. She'd left herself completely open to hurt. She'd never done that before.

And she had wanted to talk to him that night — she'd had important things to tell him.

Katie just never got the chance.

After he left her apartment, she opened a drawer in the antique dresser near the door leading to the terrace.

There was another present for Matt hidden inside.

A special present.

Katie held it in her hand, and she began to shake again. Her lips quivered, then her teeth started to chatter. She couldn't help herself, couldn't make it stop. She pulled away the wrapping paper and ribbon, and then she opened the small oblong box.

Oh, God!

61

Katie started to cry as she peered inside. The tears streamed from her eyes. The hurt she felt was almost unbearable.

She'd had something so important and so wonderful to share with Matt that night.

Inside the box was a beautiful silver baby rattle.

She was pregnant.

The Diary

Nicholas:

This is the rhythm of my life, and it is as regular and comforting as the Atlantic tides I see from the house. It is so natural, and good, and right. I know in my heart that this is where I am supposed to be.

I get up at six and take Gus for a long romp down past the Rowe farm. It opens to a field of ponies, which Gus regards with a certain laissez-faire. I think he believes they're giant golden retrievers. We eventually come out to a stretch of beach rimmed with eight- and ten-foot-high dunes and waving sea grass. Sometimes I wave back. I can be such a kook that it's embarrassing.

The route is somewhat varied, but usually we end up cutting through Mike Straw's property that has a lane of noble oaks. If it's hot or raining, the old trees act as a canopy. Gus seems to like this time of the day almost as much as I do.

What I especially like about the walks is the peaceful, easy feeling I have inside. I think a lot of it is due to the fact that I've taken back my life, reclaimed myself.

Remember the five balls, Nicky — always remember the five balls.

That is my exact thought as I start down the long road that leads home.

Just before I turn in to my driveway, I pass the Bone house next door. Melanie Bone was amazingly gracious and generous when I first moved in, supplying me with everything from helpful phone numbers to hammers, nails, paint, use of her phone, and cold, tangy lemonade, depending on the requirement. In fact, that's how I got my housepainter's number. Melanie recommended Picasso to me.

She is my age and already has four kids, God love her. I'm always in awe of anybody who can do that. All mothers are amazing. Just keeping extracurricular activities straight is like trying to run Camp Kippewa. Melanie is small, just a little over five feet, with jet black hair, and the loveliest, most welcoming smile.

Did I mention that the Bone kids are all girls? Ages one through four! I've always been bad with names, so I keep them organized by calling them by their ages. "Is Two sleeping?" "Is that Four outside on the swings?" "I think this will fit Three."

The Bones all giggle when I do this, and they think it's so silly, they've inducted Gus as honorary number five. Lord, if anyone ever overheard my system, they'd never come to see Dr. Bedford.

But they do come, Nicky, and I heal, and I am healing myself.

Now listen to what happens next. I had another date with Matt. I was invited to a party at his house.

My little man,

The house outside Vineyard Haven was beautiful, tasteful, impressive, and very expensive. I couldn't help but be impressed. As I looked around, the men and the women, even the children, arranged themselves into one demographic group: successful. It was Matt's world. It was as if the whole Upper East and West Sides of Manhattan, some smatterings of TriBeCa, and all of SoHo had been transplanted to the Vineyard. Partygoers were spread across the decks, the stone walkways, and the various gorgeously furnished rooms that opened to endless views of the sea.

The house was definitely not *me*, but I could still appreciate its beauty, even the love that had gone into making it what it was.

Matt took my arm and introduced me to his friends. Still, I felt out of place. I don't know exactly why. I had attended more than my share of events like this in Boston. Ribbon cuttings for new hospital wings, large and small cocktail soirees, the endless invitations to whatever was newsworthy in Boston.

But I really felt uncomfortable, and I didn't want to tell Matt, to spoil the night for him. My recent stint on Martha's Vineyard had been more down-home. Growing vegetables, hanging shutters, waterproofing porch floors.

At one crazy point, I actually looked down to see if I'd gotten all the white paint off my hands before I came.

You know what it was like, Nick? Sometimes when we hang together, and it's just the two of us, I'll talk Nicky-talk with you. That's the special language of made-up words; strange, funny noises; and other indecipherable codes and signals that only the two of us understand.

Then an adult will come to the door — or we'll have to go out to the market for something — and I swear I *forget* how to talk like an adult.

That's how I felt at this party. I'd spent too much time in work boots and paint-stained overalls; I was out of sync. And I liked the new rhythm I was creating for myself. Easy, simple, uncomplicated.

As I floated through a pleasant-enough haze of witty small talk and clinking crystal glasses, a little voice, *a child's voice,* broke through to me.

A small boy came running up, crying. He was probably three or four. I didn't see a parent or a nanny anywhere.

"What happened?" I bent down and asked. "Are you okay, big guy?"

"I fell," he sobbed. "Look!" And when I looked down, sure enough, his knee had a nasty scrape. There was even a little blood.

"How'd he *know* you were a doctor, Suzanne?" Matt asked.

"Children know these things," I said. "I'll take him inside and clean his knee. This white dress is meant to be chic, but maybe it looked like a doctor's lab coat to him."

I put my hand out, and the little boy reached up and took it. He told me that his name was Jack Brandon. He was the son of George and Lillian Brandon, who were at the party. He explained, in a very grown-up way, how his nanny was sick and his parents had to bring him.

As he and I emerged from the screened back door, a concerned woman came up to me.

"What happened to my son?" she asked,

and actually seemed put out.

"Jack took a little fall. We were just going to find a Band-Aid," Matt said.

"It's not serious," I said. "Just a scratch. I'm Suzanne, by the way, Suzanne Bedford."

Jack's mother acknowledged my presence with a curt nod. When she tried to take Jack's hand, he turned unexpectedly and hugged my legs.

I could tell that the mother was annoyed. She turned to a friend, and I heard her say, "What the hell does she know? It's not like she's a doctor."

Nick — listen, watch closely now, this next part is magic. There is such a thing. *Believe me.*

One night after a very long day at my office, the intrepid country doctor decided to grab a bite to eat on her way home.

I was just too tired to deal with making something, or even deciding what to make. No, Harry's Hamburger would do me just fine. A burger and fries seemed perfect to end my day. I needed a little guilty pleasure.

I guess it was a little past eight when I strolled inside. I didn't notice him at first. He was sitting by the window, eating his dinner and reading a book.

In fact, I was halfway through my burger when I saw him. Picasso, my housepainter.

I'd had very little contact with him since he left me those beautiful wildflowers in the mason jar. Occasionally, I'd hear him fixing something on the roof as I was leaving for work, or catch him painting the house, but we seldom spoke more than a few words.

I got up to pay the check. I could have walked out without saying hello because his back was turned toward me, but that seemed rude, ungracious, and snobby on my part.

I stopped at his table and asked him how he was. He was surprised to see me and asked if I'd join him for a cup of coffee, dessert, anything. It was his treat.

I gave him a lame excuse, saying I had to get home to Gus, but he was already clearing a spot for me and I just sort of sat down in his booth by the window. I liked his voice — I hadn't noticed it before. I liked his eyes, too.

"What are you reading?" I asked, feeling awkward, maybe a little scared, wanting to keep the conversation going.

"Two things . . . Melville" — he held up *Moby Dick* — "and *Trout Fishing in America.* Just in case I don't catch the big one, I have a backup."

I laughed. Picasso was pretty smart, and funny. "*Moby Dick*, hmmm, is that your summer reading or a guilt hangover because you never finished it in school?"

"Both," he admitted. "It's one of those things that you have on your to-do list in life. The book just sits there looking at you, saying, 'I'm not going away till you read me.' This is the summer I'm getting all the classics out of the way so I can finally concentrate on cheap summer thrillers."

We talked for more than an hour that night, and the time just flew. Suddenly I noticed how dark it was outside.

I looked back at him. "I have to go. I start work early in the morning."

"Me, too," he said, and smiled. "My current boss is an absolute slave driver."

I laughed. "So I've heard."

I stood up at the table and for some goony reason, I shook his hand.

"Picasso," I said, "I don't even know your real name."

"It's Matthew," he said. "Matthew Harrison."

Your father.

The next time I saw Matt Harrison, he was floating high above the world, up on my roof. He was hammering shingles like a madman, definitely a good, very conscientious worker. It was a few days after we had talked at Harry's Hamburger.

"Hey, Picasso!" I yelled, this time feeling more relaxed and even happy to see him. "You want a cold drink or something?"

"Almost done here. I'll be down in a minute. I'd love something cold."

Five minutes later he entered the cottage, as brown as a burnished copper coin.

"How's it going up there where the sea-gulls play?" I asked.

He laughed. "Good and hot! Believe it or not, I'm almost done with your roof."

Damn. Just as I was starting to like having him around.

"How's it going down here?" Matt asked me, sliding into my porch rocker in his cutoff jeans and open denim shirt. The rocker went back and bumped the trellis.

"Pretty good," I said. "No tragic headlines in the trenches today, which is always nice to report. Actually, I love my practice."

Suddenly, behind Matt, the trellis broke away from its hinges and began to tumble toward us. We both leaped up simultaneously. We managed to press the white wooden frame back into place, our heads covered with rose petals and clematis.

I began laughing as I looked over at my handyman. He looked like a bridesmaid gone wrong. He immediately responded by saying, "Oh, and you don't look like Carmen Miranda yourself?"

Matt got a hammer and nails and re-secured the trellis. My only job was to hold it steady.

I felt his strong, very solid leg brush against mine, then I could feel his chest press against my back as he hovered over me, banging in the last nail.

I shivered. *Had he done that on purpose? What was going on here?*

Our eyes met and there was a flash of something bordering on the significant between us. Whatever it was, I liked it.

Impulsively, or maybe instinctively, I asked him if he'd like to stay for dinner. "Nothing fancy. I'll throw some steaks and corn on the grill . . . like that."

He hesitated, and I wondered whether there was someone else. He certainly was good-looking enough. But my insecurity evaporated when he said, "I'm kind of grubby, Suzanne. Would you mind if I took a shower? I'd love to stay for dinner."

"There are clean towels under the sink," I told him.

And so he went to wash up and I went to make dinner. It had a nice feeling to it. Regular, simple, neighborly.

That's when I realized I didn't have any steak or corn. Fortunately, Matt never knew that I ran over to Melanie's for food . . . and that she threw in wine, candles, even half a cherry pie for dessert. She also told me that she adored Matt, that everyone did, and *good for you*.

After dinner the two of us sat talking on the front porch for a long while. The time flew again, and when I looked at my watch, I saw that it was almost eleven. I couldn't believe it.

"Tomorrow's a hospital day for me," I said. "I have early rounds."

"I'd like to reciprocate," Matt said. "Take you to dinner tomorrow? May I, Suzanne?"

I couldn't take my eyes away from his.

Matt's eyes were this incredibly gentle brown. "Yes, you absolutely may take me to dinner. I can't wait," I said. It just came out.

He laughed. "You don't have to *wait*. I'm still here, Suzanne."

"I know, and I like it, but I still can't wait for tomorrow. Good night, Matt."

He leaned forward, lightly kissed my lips, and then went home.

As it always has in my life — so far, anyway — tomorrow finally arrived. It came with Gus. Every morning he goes out to the porch and fetches the *Boston Globe*. What a retriever; what a pal!

Picasso took me around the island in his beat-up Chevy truck that afternoon, and I saw it as I never had before. I felt like a tourist. Martha's Vineyard was full of picturesque nooks and crannies and stunning views that continually surprised and delighted me.

We ended up at the lovely, multicolored Gay Head Cliffs. Matt reminded me that Tashtego in *Moby Dick* was a native harpooner and a Gay Head Indian. I guess I'd forgotten.

A couple of days later, after he'd finished some work in the house, we went for another ride.

Two days later we went out to Chappaquiddick Island. There was a tiny sign on the beach: PLEASE DON'T DISTURB, NOT EVEN THE CLAMS OR SCALLOPS. Nice. We didn't disturb anything.

I know this might sound silly, or worse, but I liked just being in the car with Matt. I looked at him and thought, *Hey I'm with this guy and he's very nice. We're out looking for an adventure.* I hadn't felt like that in a long time. I missed it.

It was at that very moment Matt turned and asked me what I was thinking about.

"Nothing. Just catching the sights," I said. I felt as if I'd just been caught doing something I wasn't supposed to.

He persisted. "If I guess right, will you tell me?"

"Sure."

"If I guess right," he said, and grinned, "then we get to have another date. Maybe even tomorrow night."

"And if you guess wrong, then we never see each other again. Big stakes riding on this."

He laughed. "Remember, I'm still painting your house, Suzanne."

"You wouldn't screw up the paint job to get even?"

Matt pretended to be offended. "I'm an artist. Picasso."

He paused before winking at me, and then

nailed his guess. "You were thinking about *us*."

I couldn't even bluff, though I did blush like crazy. "Maybe I was."

"Yes!" he shouted, and raised both arms in triumph. "And so?"

"So keep your hands on the steering wheel. And so what else?"

"So what would you like to do tomorrow?"

I started to laugh, and realized I did that a lot around him. "Boy, I have no idea. I was going to give Gus a badly needed bath, do some food shopping, maybe rent a movie. I was thinking, *The Prince of Tides*."

"Sounds great, sounds perfect. I loved Pat Conroy's book, all his stuff. Never got around to the movie. Afraid they'd mess it up. If you want some company I'd love to tag along."

I had to admit, it was great fun being with Matt. He was the polar opposite of my former Boston boyfriend, Michael Bernstein, who never seemed to do anything without a logical reason, never took a day off, probably never turned down a pretty winding road just because it was there.

Matt couldn't have been more different. He seemed to take an interest in just about everything on the planet: he was a gardener, bird-watcher, avid reader, pretty good cook, basketball player, crossword-puzzle cham-

81

pion, and, of course, he was very handy around the house.

I remember looking down at my watch at one point during our ride. But I wasn't doing it because I wanted our date to be over; I was doing it because I wanted it *not* to be over. I felt so damn happy that day. Just taking a ride with him, going absolutely nowhere.

I breathed in everything around me: the sea grass, the minty blue sky, the beach, the roaring ocean. But mostly I breathed in Matthew Harrison. His freshly laundered plaid flannel shirt, his jeans, his glistening rose-brown skin, his longish brown hair.

I breathed Matt in, held him there, and never wanted to exhale. Something very nice was happening.

Now, you may be wondering about Matt Wolfe, the lawyer? Well, I called Matt several times, but all I ever got was his answering machine, and then he never called me back. It is a small island, though, so *maybe he knew.*

Nicky,

I saw Matt Harrison every day for the next two weeks. I almost couldn't believe it. I pinched myself a lot. I smiled when no one was around.

"Have you ever ridden a horse, Suzanne?" Matt asked me on Saturday morning. "This is a serious question."

"I reckon. When I was a kid," I said with a light cowgirl drawl.

"A perfect answer — because you're about to be a kid again. Right now, today. By the way, have you ever ridden a sky blue horse that has red stripes and gold hooves?"

I looked at Matt, then shook my head. "I'd remember if I had."

"I know where there's a horse like that," he said. "In fact, I know where there are lots of them."

We drove up to Oak Bluffs, and there they were. God, what a sight.

Dozens of brightly painted stallions stood in a circle beneath the most dazzling jigsaw ceiling I'd ever seen. Hand-carved horses with flared red nostrils and black glass eyes galloped in their tireless tracks in a circle of joy.

Matthew had brought me to the Flying Horses, the oldest carousel in the country. It was still open for business, for kids of all ages.

We climbed aboard as the platform tilted and rotated beneath us, and we found perfect steeds.

As the music began, I clenched the silver horse rod, rising and falling, rising and falling. I fell under the carousel's spinning spell. Matt reached out to hold my hand and even tried to catch a kiss, which he succeeded at admirably. What a horseman!

"Where did you learn to ride like that, cowboy?" I asked as we rode up and down, but also around and around.

"Oh, I've ridden for years," Matt said. "Took lessons here when I was three. You see that blue stallion up ahead? Blue the color of the sky? Wild-blue-yonder blue?"

"Reckon I do."

"He threw me a couple of times. Man, did I take a nasty spill or two. That's why I wanted to make sure you got National

Velvet first time out. She's got an even temper, lovely coat of shellac."

"She's beautiful, Matt. You know, when I was a kid I did ride some. It's all coming back to me. I used to go riding with my grandfather out in Goshen, New York. Funny I should remember that now."

Good memories are like charms, Nicky. Each is special. You collect them, one by one, until one day you look back and discover they make a long, colorful bracelet.

By the end of that day, I would have my first in a series of beautiful charms about Matthew Harrison.

Katie

Katie would never forget the very first time she saw Matt Harrison. It was in her small, comfortable office at the publishing house, and she had been looking forward to the meeting for days. She had loved *Songs of a Housepainter*, which seemed to her like the most memorable short stories, quite magical, condensed into powerful, very moving poems. He wrote about everyday life — tending a garden, painting a house, burying a beloved dog, having a child — but his *choice* of words distilled life so perfectly. She was still amazed that she had discovered his work.

And then he walked through the door of her office, and she was even more amazed. No, make that *entranced*. The most primitive parts of her brain and nervous system locked on to the image before her — the poet, *the man*. Katie felt her heart skip a beat, and she thought, *My, my. Careful, careful.*

He was taller than she was — she guessed about six foot two. He had a good nose and strong-looking chin, and everything about his face held together extremely well, like one of his poems. His hair was longish, sandy brown, clean and lustrous. He had a deep working-man's tan. He smiled at something, hopefully not her height or her gawkiness or the goofy look on her face — but she liked him, anyway. What was there not to like?

They had dinner that night, and he gallantly let her buy. He did insist on picking up the tab for a couple of glasses of expensive port a little later. Then they went to a jazz club on the Upper West Side, on a "school night" as Katie called her work nights. He finally dropped her off at her apartment at three in the morning, apologized profusely and sincerely, gave her the sweetest kiss on the cheek, and then off he went in a cab.

Katie stood on the front steps and was finally able to catch her breath, maybe for the first time since he had walked through the door of her office. She tried to remember . . . *was Matthew Harrison married?*

He was back in her office the following morning — to work — but the two of them skedaddled off to lunch at noon and didn't return for the rest of the day. They went museum hopping, and he certainly knew his art. He didn't show off, but he easily knew as much as Katie did. She kept thinking — who *is* this guy? And why am I allowing myself to feel the way I'm feeling?

And then — *why am I not trying to feel like this all the time?*

He came up to her place that night, and she continued to be astonished that any of this was happening. Katie was infamous with her friends for *not* sleeping around, for being too romantic, and way too old-fashioned about sex; but here she was with this good-looking, undeniably sexy, housepainter-poet from Martha's Vineyard, and she couldn't *not* be with him. He never, ever hustled her — in fact, he seemed almost as surprised about being in her apartment as she was that he was there.

"Hummuna, hummuna," Katie said, and they both laughed nervously.

"My sentiments exactly," Matt said.

They went to bed for the first time on that rainy night, and he made her notice the music of the raindrops as they fell on her street, the rooftop, and even the trees outside her apartment. It was beautiful, it was music; but soon they had forgotten the patter of the rain, and everything else, except for the urgent touch of each other.

He was so natural and easy and good in

bed that it scared Katie a little. It was as if he had known her for a long time. He knew how to hold her, how and where to touch her, how to wait, and then when to let everything on the inside explode. She loved the way he touched her, the gentle way he kissed her lips, her cheeks, the hollow of her throat, her back, breasts — well, everywhere.

"You're absolutely ravishing, and you don't know it, do you?" he whispered to her, then smiled. "You have the most delicate body. Your eyes are gorgeous. And I *love* your braid."

"You and my mother," Katie said. She loosened the braid and let her long hair cascade over her shoulders.

"Hmmm. I love that look, too," Matt said, and winked at her.

When he finally left her apartment the next morning, Katie had the feeling that she had never been with anyone like that, never experienced such intimacy with another person. *My God, why not?* she asked herself.

She kind of missed Matt already. It was insane, completely ridiculous, not *her;* but she *did* miss him. *My God, why not?*

When she got to her office that morning, he was already there, waiting for her. Her heart nearly stopped.

"We'd better do some work," she said.

"Seriously, Matthew."

He didn't say a word, just shut her office door and kissed her until Katie felt as if she were melting into the hardwood floor.

He finally pulled away, looked into her eyes again, and said, "As soon as I left your place, *I missed you.*"

The Diary

Nicholas,

I remember all of this as if it happened yesterday. It's still vibrant and alive. Matt and I were riding on the Edgartown–Vineyard Haven road in my Jeep. Gus went along for the ride. He sat on the backseat and looked like one of the lions that guard the front of the New York Public Library.

"Can't you drive any faster?" Matt asked, tapping his fingers on the dashboard. "I walk faster than this."

I am by my own admission a slow and careful driver. Matt had found my first flaw.

"Hey I got the safety-first award in my driver's ed class in Cornwall on Hudson. I hung the diploma under my medical degree."

Matt laughed and rolled his brown eyes. He got all of my dumb little jokes.

We were driving to his mother's house. Matt thought it would be interesting for me to meet her.

Interesting? What did that mean?

"Oops, there's my mom!" Matt said just then. "Oh, man. There she is."

She was up on the roof of the house when we got there. She was fixing an ancient TV antenna. We got out of my old blue Jeep, and Matt called up to her.

"Mom, this is Suzanne. And Gus the Wonder Dog. Suzanne . . . my mother, Jean. She taught me how to fix things around the house."

His mother was tall, lanky, silver-haired. She called down to us, "Very nice to meet you, Suzanne. You, too, Gus. You three go have a seat on the porch. I'll only be a minute up here."

"If you don't fall off the roof and break both your legs," Matt said. "Fortunately, we have a good doctor in the house."

"I won't fall off the roof." Jean laughed, and went back to her work. "I only fall off extension ladders."

Matt and I took our seats at a wrought-iron table on the porch. Gus preferred the front yard. The house was an old saltbox with a northern view of the harbor. To the south lay cornfields, and then deep woods that gave you the impression you were in Maine.

"It's gorgeous here. Is this where you grew up?" I asked.

98

"No, I was born in Edgartown. This house was bought a few years after my father died."

"I'm sorry, Matt."

He shrugged. "It's another thing we have in common, I guess."

"So why didn't you tell me?" I asked him.

He smiled. "You know, I guess I just don't like to talk a lot about sad things. Now you know *my* flaw. What good does it do to talk about sad things in the past?"

Jean suddenly appeared with iced tea and a plate heaped with chocolate-chip cookies.

"Well, I promise I won't give you the once-over, Suzanne. We're too mature for that sort of thing," she said with a quick wink. "I would love to hear about your practice, though. Matthew's father was a doctor, you know."

I looked over at him. Matt hadn't told me that, either. "My dad died when I was eight years old. I don't remember too much."

"He's private about some things, Suzanne. Matthew was hurt badly when his dad died. Don't listen to him on that. I think he believes it might make other people uncomfortable to hear about how much he hurts."

She winked at Matt; he winked back at her. I could tell they were close. It was nice to see. Sweet.

"So, tell me about yourself, Jean. Unless

you're a private person, too."

"Hell, no!" she said with a laugh. "I'm an open book. What do you want to know?"

It turned out that Jean was a local artist — a painter. She walked me through the cottage and showed me some of her work. She was good, too. I knew enough to be fairly sure that her paintings could have sold at a lot of galleries in Back Bay, or even New York. Jean had framed a quote from the primitive artist Grandma Moses. It said, "I paint from the top down. From the sky, then the mountains, then the hills, then the cattle, and then the people."

Jean laughed at my praise of her work and said, "I once saw a cartoon with a couple standing before a Jackson Pollock painting. The painting had a price tag of a million dollars under it, and the man turned to the woman and said, 'Well, he comes through clear enough on the price.' " She had a good sense of humor about her work, about anything really. I saw a lot of her in Matt.

The afternoon turned into evening, and Matt and I ended up staying for dinner. There was even time to see a priceless old album of some of Matt's baby pictures.

He was a *cutie*, Nick. He had your blond hair as a boy and that spunky look you have sometimes.

"No naked bottoms on bear rugs?" I asked Jean as I went through the pictures.

She laughed. "Look hard enough, and I'm sure you'll find one. He has a nice butt. If you haven't seen it, you should ask for a look."

I laughed. Jean was a hoot.

"All right," Matt said, "show's over. Time to hit the highway."

"We were just getting into the good stuff," Jean said, and made a pouty face. "You are a party pooper."

It was about eleven when we finally got up to leave. Jean grabbed me in a hug.

She whispered against my cheek, "He never ever brings anybody home. So whatever you think of him, he must like you a lot. Please don't hurt him. He *is* sensitive, Suzanne. And he's a pretty good guy."

"Hey!" Matt finally called from the car. "Knock it off, you two."

"Too late," his mother said. "The damage is already done. I had to spill the beans. Suzanne knows enough to drop you like a bad habit."

The damage was probably already done — to me. I was falling for Matthew Harrison. I couldn't quite believe it myself, but it was happening, if it hadn't already happened.

The Hot Tin Roof is a fun nightclub at the Martha's Vineyard Airport in Edgartown. Matt and I went there to eat oysters and listen to the blues on Friday night. At that point, I would have gone anywhere with him.

A host of local celebrities floated in and out of the bar: funky, laid-back Carly Simon, Tom Paxton, William Styron and his wife, Rose. Matt thought it would be fun to sit at the raw bar and just people watch. It was, too.

"Want to slow dance?" Matt asked me after we'd had our fill of oysters and cold beer.

"Dance? No one is dancing, Matt. I don't think this is a dancing-type place."

"This is my favorite song, and I'd love to

dance with you. Will you dance with me, Suzanne?"

I did something I do infrequently. I blushed.

"Come on," Matt whispered against my cheek. "No one will tell the other doctors at the hospital."

"All right. One dance."

"Done well, one dance will always lead to another," he said.

We began to slow dance in our little corner of the bar. Eyes started to turn our way. What was I doing? What had happened to me? Whatever it was, it felt so good to be doing it.

"Is this okay?" Matt checked.

"You know, actually it's great. What is this song, anyway? You said it was your favorite."

"Oh, I have no idea, Suzanne. I just wanted an excuse to hold you close."

With that, Matt held me a little tighter. I loved being in his arms. I loved, loved, loved it. Corny maybe, but absolutely true. What can I say? I felt a little dizzy as we spun around in rhythm with the music.

"I have a question to ask you," he whispered against the side of my ear.

"Okay," I whispered back.

"How do you feel about us? So far?"

I kissed him. "Like that."

He smiled. "That's how I feel, too."

"Good."

"I lived with somebody for three years," Matt said. "We met while we were at Brown. The Vineyard wasn't right for her, but it was for me."

"Four years. Another doctor," I confessed.

Matt leaned in and lightly kissed me on the lips again. "Would you come home with me tonight, Suzanne?" he asked. "I want to do some more dancing."

I told him I would love to.

I have this wink that Matt calls "Suzanne's famous wink." I did it for the first time to Matt that night. He loved it.

Matt's house was a small Victorian covered in gingerbread lace that draped itself over the eaves and softened all the corners. The trellises, railings, and overhangs looked as if they'd been lifted off some elaborately trimmed wedding cake and carefully placed around the rim of the roof.

It was the first time I had been invited, and I was suddenly nervous. My mouth was cottony and dry. I hadn't been with anyone like this since Michael, and that was still a bad memory for me.

We went inside and I immediately noticed a library. The room had been remodeled to be made up of nothing but shelves. There were thousands of books in there. My eyes traveled up and down the bookshelves: Scott Fitzgerald, John Cheever, Virginia Woolf, Anaïs Nin, Thomas Merton, Doris Lessing. An entire wall was devoted to collections of poetry. W. H. Auden, Wallace Stevens, Hart Crane, Sylvia Plath, James

Wright, Elizabeth Bishop, Robert Hayden, and many, many more. There was an antique globe; an old English pond boat, its sails stained and listing; some nautical brass fittings; a big pine table covered in writing pads and miscellaneous papers.

"I love this room. Can I look around?" I asked.

"I love it, too. Of course you can look."

I was totally surprised by the cover page on top of a stack of pages. It read, *Songs of a Housepainter*, Poems by Matthew Harrison.

Matt was a poet? He hadn't told me about it. He really didn't like to talk about himself, did he? What other secrets did he have?

"Okay, yes," he admitted quietly. "I do some scribbling. That's all it is. I've had the bug since I was sixteen, and I've been trying to work it out since I left Brown. I majored in English and Housepainting. Just kidding. You ever write, Suzanne?"

"No, not really," I said. "But I've been thinking about starting a diary."

In the south of France there is supposedly a special time known as the Night of the Falling Stars. On this night, everything is just so. Perfect and magical. According to the French, the stars seem to pour out of the sky, like cream from a pitcher.

It was like that for us; there were so many stars, I could imagine I was up in heaven.

Matt said, "Let's take a walk down to the beach. Okay? I have an idea."

"I've noticed that you have a lot of ideas."

"Maybe it's the poet in me."

He grabbed an old blanket, his CD player, and a bottle of champagne. We walked on a winding path through high sea grass, finally finding a patch of sand to spread the blanket.

Matt popped open the champagne, and it sparkled and blinked in the midnight air. Then he pushed PLAY and the strains of Debussy whirled up into the starry night sky.

Matt and I danced again, and we were in another time and place. Around and around we went, in sync with the rhythm of the sea, turning up fountains of sand, leaving improbable footprint patterns in our wake. I let my fingers play on his back, his neck. I let my hands comb through his hair.

"I didn't know you could waltz," I said.

He laughed. "I didn't know, either."

It was late when we made our way back up from the beach, but I wasn't tired. If anything, I was more awake than ever. I was still dancing, flying, singing inside. I hadn't expected any of this to happen. Not now, maybe not ever. It seemed a thousand years from my heart attack in the Public Garden in Boston.

Nicky, I felt so lucky — so blessed.

Matt gently took my hand and led me up the stairs to his room. I wanted to go with him, but still I was afraid. I hadn't done this in a while.

Neither of us spoke, but suddenly my mouth opened wide. He had converted the top floor to one big, beautiful space, complete with skylights that seemed to absorb the evening sky. I loved what he had done to the room. He turned on the CD player in the bedroom.

Sarah Vaughan. Perfect.

Matt told me that he could count falling stars from his bed. "One night I counted sixteen. A personal record."

He came to me, slowly and deliberately, drawing me toward him like a magnet. I could feel the buttons in the back of my blouse coming undone. The little hairs on the back of my neck stood on end. His fingers traveled down to the base of my spine, playing so very gently. He slipped off my blouse, and I watched it float to the floor, milkweed in a breeze.

I stood so close to him, felt so close to Matt, barely breathing, feeling light, dizzy, magical, and very special.

He slipped his hands down onto my hips. Matt then leaned me back, gently laid me on his bed. I watched him in the moon shadows. I found him to be beautiful. *How had this happened? Why was I suddenly so lucky?*

He stretched over me like a quilt on a cold night. That's all I will say of it, all I will write.

Dear Nicky,

I hope when you grow up that everything you want comes your way, but especially love. When it's true, when it's right, love can give you the kind of joy that you can't get from any other experience. I have been in love; I *am* in love, so I speak from experience. I have also lived long periods without love in my life, and there is no way to describe the difference between the two.

We is always so much better than *I*.

Please don't listen to anyone who tells you otherwise. And don't ever become a cynic, Nicky. Anything but that!

I look at your little hands and feet. I count your toes over and over, moving them gently as if they were beads on an abacus. I kiss your belly till you laugh. You are so innocent. Stay that way when it comes to love.

Just look at you. How is it that I got so lucky? I got the perfect one. Your nose and mouth are just right. Your eyes and your smile are your very best features. Already I see your personality blossoming. It's in your eyes. What are you thinking about right now? The mobile over your head? Your music box? Daddy says you're probably thinking about girls and tools and flashy cars. He jokes that your favorite things are flashy cars, pretty girls, and birthday cake. "He's a real boy, Suzanne."

That's true, and it's probably a good thing. But do you know what you like the best? Teddy bears. You're so gentle and sweet with your little bears.

Daddy and I laugh about all the good things that wait for you. But what we want most for you is love and that it will always surround you. It is a gift. If I can, I will try to teach you how to receive such a gift. Because to be without love is to be without grace, what matters most in life.

We is so much better than *I*.

If you need proof, just look at *us*.

"It's Matt. Hi. Hello? Anybody home? Suzanne? You here?"

The banging at my kitchen door was persistent and annoying, like an unexpected visit from an out-of-town relative. I went to the door, opened it, and then stopped, my mouth open in a little circle of surprise.

It was Matt, all right, but not Matt Harrison.

My visitor was Matt Wolfe.

Behind him in my driveway, I could see his glistening green Jag convertible.

Where had he been? He *still* hadn't returned any of my calls.

"Hi," he said. "God, you look good, Suzanne. You look great, actually." He leaned in and I let him give me a kiss on the cheek.

I had no reason to feel guilty — but I did, anyway. "Matt. How are you? I just made some sun tea. Come on in."

And he did, finding a comfy, sunny place in the kitchen, leaning into what looked like a catch-up mode. We definitely had some catching up to do, didn't we?

"I've been out of town for most of the month, Suzanne. I kept meaning to call, but I was in the middle of a legal fiasco. Unfortunately, it was in Thailand."

Suddenly he smiled. "And you know — blah, blah, blah, yadda, yadda, yah. So how have you been? Obviously, you got some sun. You look fantastic."

"Well, thanks . . . so do you."

I had to tell him. I even decided to give Matt Wolfe the long version of what had been happening in my life.

He listened, smiling at some parts, fidgeting nervously at others. I could tell his acceptance was somewhat bittersweet. But he kept listening intently, and when I was done, he got off the kitchen stool, put his arms around me, and gave me a hug.

"Suzanne," he said, "I'm happy for you."

He smiled bravely. "I knew in my gut I shouldn't have gone away. Now the best thing that could have happened to me has slipped through my fingers again."

I found myself laughing. I was starting to notice that Matt Wolfe was a little bit of a con man. "Oh, Matt, your flattery is so sweet. Thanks for being a friend. Thanks for being *you*."

"Hey, if I'm gonna lose the big prize, I'm going down with a little dignity. But I'm telling you, Suzie, if this guy flinches, or if I sense a crack in the dam, I'm coming back."

We both laughed, and I walked him out to the Jag. Somehow, I just knew that Matt would be all right. I doubted he'd been all by his lonesome in Thailand. And let's face it, he hadn't called in nearly a month.

I watched Matt get into his car, his pride and joy.

"I actually think you two will get along. In fact, I think the two Matts will like each other a lot," I called from the porch.

"Oh, great! Now I have to like the guy, too?" he called back.

The last thing I heard him say before he fired the convertible's powerful engine was, "He does know how to duel, doesn't he?"

"Okay What's going on? Spill the beans, Suzanne. I want the scoop. I know there's something going on with you," said my neighbor and friend Melanie Bone. "I feel it in my *bones*."

She was right. I hadn't told her how Matt and I were progressing, but she could read my face and maybe even tell by the spring in my step.

We were walking along the beach near our houses, the kids and Gus romping in front of us.

"You're smart," I told her. "And nosy."

"I know that already. So tell me what I don't know. *Spill*."

I couldn't resist any longer. It had to come out sooner or later. "I'm in love, Mel. This has never happened before. I'm head over heels in love with Matt Harrison. I have no idea what's to become of us!"

She screeched. Then Melanie jumped up and down a few times in the sand. She was so cute, and such a good friend. She screeched again.

"That is so perfect, Suzanne. I knew he was a good painter, but I had no idea about his other talents."

"Did you know he's a poet? A very good poet."

"No, you're kidding," she said.

"A beautiful dancer?"

"That doesn't surprise me. He moves pretty well on rooftops. So, how did this happen? I mean, how did it go from adding a touch of Cape Cod white to your house to *this?*"

I started to giggle and felt like a schoolgirl. After all, things like this didn't happen to grown women.

"I talked to him one night at the hamburger place."

Melanie arched an eyebrow. "*Okay.* You talked to him at the hamburger place?"

"I can talk to Matt about anything, Melanie. I've never had that happen with any man before. He even writes poems the way he talks. It's very down-to-earth and at the same time, sometimes over your head. He's passionate, exciting. He's humble, too. Maybe more than he should be sometimes."

Melanie suddenly gave me hug. "God, Suzanne, this is it! As IT as it can get. Congratulations, you're *gone for good.*"

We laughed like a couple of giddy fifteen-year-olds, and headed back with Melanie's kids and Gus. That morning at her house, we talked nonstop about everything from first dates to first pregnancies. Melanie confessed that she was thinking of having a fifth baby, which blew me away. For her it was as easy as organizing a cabinet. She had her life as under control as a grocery shelf lined neatly with canned goods. Orderly, alphabetized, well stocked.

I also fantasized about having kids that morning, Nicholas. I knew I would have a high-risk pregnancy because of my heart condition, but I didn't care. Maybe there was something in me that knew you'd be here one day. A flutter of hope. A deep desire. Or just the sheer inevitability of what love between two people can bring.

You — it brought you.

Bad stuff happens, Nicholas. Sometimes it makes no sense at all. Sometimes it's unfair. Sometimes it just plain sucks.

The red pickup came tearing around the corner, going close to sixty, but the whole thing seemed to happen in slow motion.

Gus was crossing the street, heading toward the beach, where he likes to race the surf and bark at seagulls. Bad timing.

I saw the whole thing. I opened my mouth to stop him, but it was probably already too late.

The pickup swung around the blind curve like a blur. I could almost smell the rubber of the tires as they skidded along the hot tar, then I watched as the left front fender caught Gus.

A second more, and he would have cleared that unforgiving metal.

Five miles an hour slower, and the pickup would have missed him.

Or maybe if Gus had been a couple of

years younger, closer to his prime, it wouldn't have happened.

The timing was nightmarish, irrevocable, like a rock falling on the windshield of a passing car.

It was over, done, and Gus lay like a rag discarded by the side of the road. It was so sad. He'd been so defenseless, so carefree just seconds before as he romped toward the water.

"No!" I yelled. The truck had stopped, and two stubble-faced men in their twenties got out. They both wore colorful bandannas on their heads. They stared at what their speeding vehicle had done.

"Gee, I'm sorry, I didn't see him," the driver stammered, and hitched at his blue jeans as he looked at poor Gus.

I didn't have time to think, to argue, to yell at him. The only thing I needed to do was to get Gus help.

I threw the driver my keys. "Open the back of my Jeep," I snapped as I gently lifted Gus up into my arms. He was limp and heavy, but still breathing, still *Gus*.

I laid him in the back of the Jeep, bloody and tenuous. His sweet, familiar eyes were as far away as the clouds. Then he focused on me. Gus whimpered pitifully, and my heart broke into a hundred pieces.

"Don't die, Gus," I whispered. "Hold on, boy," I said as I pulled out of my driveway. "Please don't leave me."

I called Matt on my cell phone, and he met me at the vet's. Dr. Pugatch took Gus in at once, maybe because she saw the look of desperation on my face.

"The truck was going way too fast, Matt," I told him. I was reliving the scene again, and I could see every detail. Matt was even angrier than me.

"It's that damn curve. Every time you pull out, I worry about it. I need to lay you a new driveway on the other side of the house. That way you'll be able to see the road."

"This is so horrible. Gus was right there when I —" I stopped myself. I still hadn't told Matt about my heart attack. Gus knew, but Matt didn't.

I had to tell him soon.

"Shhhh, it's okay, Suzanne. It's going to be okay." Matt held me, and though it wasn't okay, it was as good as it could possibly be. I burrowed into his chest and stayed there. Then I could feel Matt shaking a little. He and Gus had become close, too. Matt had unofficially taken over most of the ball playing with Gus.

Two hours later the vet came out. It seemed like an eternity before she spoke.

Now I knew how my own patients must feel when I hesitate or am at a loss for words. Their faces seem calm but their bodies convey something else. They beg to be relieved of their anxiety with good news, *only good news.*

"Suzanne, Matt . . . ," Dr. Pugatch finally said. "I'm sorry. I'm so, so sorry. Gus didn't make it."

I began to cry, and my whole body was shaking uncontrollably. Gus had always been there with me, for me. He was my good buddy, my roommate, my jogging partner, my confidant. We had been together for fourteen years.

Bad stuff does happen sometimes, Nicholas.

Always remember that, but remember that you have to move on, somehow.

You just pick your head up and stare at something beautiful like the sky, or the ocean, and you move the hell on.

Nicholas,

An unexpected letter arrived in the mail for me the next day.

I don't know why I didn't rip it open and read it. I just stood there wondering why Matt Harrison had written me a letter when he could easily have picked up the phone or come over.

I stood at the end of the driveway in front of the weatherbeaten, off-white mailbox. I opened the letter carefully and held it tight so it wouldn't be blown away by the ocean wind.

Rather than try to paraphrase what the letter said, Nicky, I'm enclosing it in the diary.

Dear Suzanne,

You are the explosion of carnations
   in a dark room.
Or the unexpected scent of pine
   miles from Maine.

You are a full moon
that gives midnight its meaning.
And the explanation of water
For all living things.

You are a compass,
a sapphire,
a bookmark.
A rare coin,
a smooth stone,
a blue marble.

You are an old lore,
a small shell,
a saved silver dollar.
You are a fine quartz,
a feathered quill,
and a fob from a favorite watch.

You are a valentine
tattered and loved and reread a
    hundred times.
You are a medal found in the drawer
    of a once sung hero.
You are honey
and cinnamon
and West Indies spices,
lost from the boat
that was once Marco Polo's.

You are a pressed rose,
a pearl ring,
and a red perfume bottle found near
   the Nile.

You are an old soul from an ancient
   place,
a thousand years, and centuries and
   millenniums ago.

And you have traveled all this way
   just so I could love you.
I do.

                              Matt

   What can I say, Nicholas, that your good,
sweet father cannot say better? He is a stun-
ningly good writer, and I'm not even sure he
knows it.
   I love him so much.
   Who wouldn't?

Nicky,

I called Matt very early the next morning, as soon as I dared, about seven. I had been up since a little past four, thinking that I had to call him, even rehearsing what I should say and how I should say it. I don't really know how to be dishonest or manipulate people very well. It puts me at a great disadvantage sometimes.

This was hard.

This was impossible.

"Matt, hi. It's Suzanne. Hope I'm not calling too early. Can you come by tonight?" was all I could manage.

"Of course I can. In fact, I was going to call you and ask for a date."

Matt arrived at the house a little past seven that night. He was wearing a yellow plaid shirt and navy blue trousers — kind of formal for him.

"You want to take a walk on the beach, Suzanne? Take in the sunset with me?"

It was exactly what I wanted to do. He'd read my mind.

As soon as we crossed the beach road and had our bare feet in the still-warm sand, I said, "Can I talk? There's something I have to tell you."

He smiled. "Sure. I always like the sound of your voice."

Poor Matt. I doubted that he was going to like the sound of what was coming next.

"There's something I've wanted to tell you for a while. I keep putting it off. I'm not even sure how to broach the subject now."

He took my hand, swung it gently in rhythm with our strides. "Consider it broached. Go ahead, Suzanne."

"Why are you so dressed up tonight?" I thought to ask him.

"I'm dressed up because I have a date with the most special woman on this entire island. Is that the subject you had trouble broaching?"

I squeezed his hand a little. "Not exactly. No, it isn't. Okay, here goes."

Matt finally said, "You are scaring me a little now."

"Sorry," I whispered. "*Sorry*. Matt, right before I came to the Vineyard —"

"You had a heart attack," he said in the softest voice. "You almost died in the Public

Garden, but you didn't, thank God. And now, here we are, and I think we're two of the luckiest people. I know that *I* am. I'm here holding your hand, looking into your beautiful blue eyes."

I stopped walking and stared at Matt in disbelief. The setting sun was just over his shoulder, and it looked like a nimbus. Was Matthew an angel?

"How long have you known? *How* did you know?" I stammered.

"I heard before I came to work for you. This is a small island, Suzanne. I was half expecting some old biddy with a walker."

"I *did* use a walker for a couple of days in Boston. I had surgery. So you knew, but you never told me you knew."

"I didn't think it was my place. I knew that you'd tell me when you were ready. I guess you're ready, Suzanne. That's good news. I've been thinking about what happened to you a lot in the past few weeks. I even arrived at a point of view. Would you like to hear it?"

I held on to Matt's arm. "Of course I would."

"Well, I can't help thinking of this whenever we're together. I think, isn't it lucky that Suzanne didn't die in Boston and we have today to be together. Now we get to watch this sunset. Or isn't it lucky Suzanne didn't die and we're sitting out on her front porch playing hearts or watching a stupid Red Sox game. Or listening to Mozart or even that smarmy love song you like by Savage Garden. I keep thinking, isn't this day, this moment, incredibly special, because you're *here*, Suzanne."

I started to cry, and that's when Matt took me into his arms. We cuddled on the beach for a long time, and I never wanted him to let me go. Never ever. We fit together so well. I kept thinking, *Isn't this moment incredibly special? Aren't I the lucky one?*

"Suzanne?" I heard him whisper, and I felt Matt's warm breath on my cheek.

"I'm here. Hard to miss. I'm right here in your arms. I'm not going anywhere."

"That's good. I want you to always be there. I love having you in my arms. Now there's something I have to say. Suzanne, I love you so much. I treasure everything about you. I miss you when we're apart for just a couple of hours. Every day while I'm working, I can't wait to see you that night. I've been looking for you for a long time, I just didn't know it. But now I do. Suzanne, will you marry me?"

I pulled back and looked into the beautiful eyes of this precious man I had found somehow, or maybe who had found me. I couldn't stop smiling, and the warm glow spreading inside me was the most incredible feeling.

"I love you, Matt. I've been looking for you for a long time, too. Yes, I'll marry you."

Katie

Katie closed the diary again.

She slammed it shut this time. It hurt her so much to read these pages. She could take them only in small doses. Matt had warned her in his letter that it might happen, and it had. *There will be parts that may be hard for you to read.* What an incredible understatement that was.

The diary continued to put her in a place of unexpected surprises. Now it was making her jealous, something she didn't think she was capable of. She *was* jealous of Suzanne. She kind of felt like a jerk, a small and petty person. Not herself. Maybe it was hormones. Or maybe it was just a normal reaction to everything abnormal that had happened to her recently.

She shut her eyes tight, and felt incredibly alone. She hugged herself with both arms. She needed to talk to someone besides Guinevere and Merlin. Ironically, the person she wanted to reach out to was on Martha's

Vineyard. As much as she wanted to, she wouldn't call him. She would call her friends Laurie or Gilda or Susan, but not Matt.

Her eyes moved over to the bookshelves she had built into her walls. Her apartment was like a small bookstore. Very independent. *Orlando, The Age of Innocence, Bella Tuscany, Harry Potter and the Goblet of Fire, The God of Small Things.* She'd been reading voraciously ever since she was seven or eight. She read everything, anything.

She was feeling a little queasy again. Cold, too. She wrapped herself in a blanket and watched *Ally McBeal* on TV. Ally turned thirty in the episode, and Katie cried. She wasn't nearly as crazy as Ally and her friends, but the show still hit a nerve.

She lay on her living-room couch and couldn't stop thinking about the baby growing inside her. "It's all right, little baby," she whispered. *I hope so, anyway.*

Katie remembered the night when she had gotten pregnant. She'd had a fantasy in bed that night, but she dismissed it, thinking, *I've never gotten pregnant before.* She hadn't ever missed a period — except one time in college, when she'd been playing varsity basketball at North Carolina and learned that her body fat was too low.

That last night with Matt, Katie had felt

134

that it had never been like this before. Something had changed between them.

She could feel it in the way he held her and looked at her with his luminous brown eyes. She felt some of his walls come down, felt, *This is it.* He was ready to tell her things that he hadn't been able to talk about.

Had that scared Matt? Had he felt it, too, that last night we were together? Was that what had happened?

She had never felt as close to Matt as she had that night. She always loved being with him, but that night it was urgent; they were both so needy.

Katie recalled that it had started so simply: all he had done was wrap his fingers around hers. He slid his free arm beneath her and stared into her eyes. Next their legs touched, then their entire bodies reached toward each other. She and Matt never lost eye contact, and it seemed as if they were really one in a way that they hadn't been before that night.

His eyes said, *I love you, Katie.* She couldn't have been wrong about that.

She had always wanted it to be like that, *just like that.* She'd had that thought, that dream, a thousand times before it actually happened. His strong arms were around her back, and her long legs were wrapped around his. She knew she could never forget any of those images or sensations.

He was so light when he was on top of her, supporting himself on his elbows, his knees. He was athletic, graceful, giving, dominating. He whispered her name over and over: *Katie, sweet Katie, my Katie, Katie, Katie.*

This was it, she knew — he was completely aware and attuned to her, and she had never experienced such love with anyone before. She loved it, loved Matt, and she pulled him deep inside, where they made a baby.

Katie knew what she had to do the next morning. *Seven A.M.* — but it wasn't too early for this. This was it.

She called home — Asheboro, nestled between the Blue Ridge and Great Smoky Mountains in North Carolina — where life had always been simpler. Kinder, too. Much, much kinder.

So why had she left Asheboro? she wondered as the phone began to ring. To follow her love of books? It was her passion, something she truly loved. Or had she just needed to see a world larger than the one she knew in the heart of North Carolina?

"Hey, Katie," her mother answered on the third ring. "You're up with the city birds this morning. How are you doing, sweetie?"

They had Caller ID in Asheboro now. Everything was changing, wasn't it? For better or for worse, or maybe somewhere in between.

"Hey, Mom. What's the latest?"

"You doing a little better today?" her mother asked. She knew that Katie had found someone in New York. She knew all about Matt and had loved it when Katie called to talk about him, especially when she said they would probably be getting married. Now he had left her, and Katie was suffering. She didn't deserve that. Her mother had tried to get her to come home, but Katie wouldn't do it. She was too tough — right. A big-city girl. Well, her mother knew better.

"Some. Yeah, sure. Well, actually, no. I'm still a *mess*. I'm *pitiful*. I'm *hopeless*. I swore I'd never let a man get me into a state like this — and here I am."

Katie began to tell her mother about the diary and what she had read so far. The lesson of the five balls. Suzanne's daily routine on Martha's Vineyard. How she met Matt Wolfe again.

"You know what's so strange, Mom? I actually like Suzanne. Damn it. I'm such a sap. I ought to hate her, but I can't do it."

"Of course you can't. Well, at least this dumb bunny Matt has good taste in women," her mother said, and cackled as she always did. She could be wicked-funny when she wanted to be. Katie was always grateful that she'd inherited her mom's sense of humor. But she didn't feel like joking.

Tell her, Katie was thinking to herself. *Tell her everything.*

But she couldn't. She had told her two best friends in New York — Laurie Raleigh and Susan Kingsolver — but couldn't tell her mother she was pregnant. The words just wouldn't come out of her mouth.

Why not? Katie wondered. But she knew the answer. She didn't want to hurt her mother and father. They meant too much to her.

Her mom was quiet for a moment. Holly Wilkinson was still a first-grade teacher in Asheboro, Katie's mentor for thirty years. She was always, *always* there for her, supportive, even when Katie had gone to dreaded, hated New York and her father didn't talk to her for a month.

Tell her, Katie. She'll understand. She can help you.

But Katie just couldn't get the words out. She choked on them and felt bile rising from her stomach.

Katie and her mother talked for almost an hour, and then she spoke to her father. She was almost as close to him as she was to her mom. He was a minister, much beloved in the area because he taught "God-loving" instead of "God-fearing." The only time he'd ever been really mad at Katie was when she had packed up and moved to New York. But he got over it, and he never threw it up in her face anymore.

Her mother and father were like that. Good people. And so was she, Katie thought, and knew it was true. *Good people.*

So why had Matt left her? How could he just walk out of her life? And what was the diary supposed to tell her that would somehow make her understand?

What was the deep, dark secret of the diary? That Matt had a smart, wonderful wife and a beautiful, darling child and that he had slipped up with her? Had an affair with a New York woman? Strayed for the first time in his picture-perfect marriage? *Damn him! Damn him!*

When she had finished talking to her dad, Katie sat in her study with her good buddies Guinevere and Merlin; they curled up on the couch with her and looked out the bay window at the Hudson. She loved the river, the way it changed every day or even several times in the same day. The river was a lesson, just like the lesson of the five balls.

"What should I do?" she whispered to Guinevere and Merlin. Tears welled up in her eyes, then spilled down her cheeks.

Katie picked up the phone again. She sat there nervously tapping the receiver with her fingernail. It took all the courage that she had, but she finally dialed the number.

Katie almost hung up — but she waited through ring after ring. Finally, she got the answering machine.

She choked up when she actually heard a voice. "This is Matt. Your message is important to me. Please leave it at the beep. Thanks."

Katie left a message. She hoped it was important to Matt. "I'm reading the diary," she said. That was all.

The Diary

Come to our wedding, Nicky. This is your invitation. I want you to know exactly what it was like on the day your mother and father pledged their love.

Snow was falling gently on the island. The bells were ringing in the clear, cold, crisp December air as dozens of frosty well-wishers crossed the threshold into the Gay Head Community Church, which happens to be the oldest Indian Baptist church in the country. It's also one of the loveliest.

There is only one word that can describe our wedding day . . . *joy*. Matt and I were both giddy. I was just about flying among the angels carved in the four corners of the chapel ceiling.

I really did feel like an angel, in an antique white dress strung with a hundred luminescent pearls. My grandfather came to Martha's Vineyard for the first time in fifteen years, just to walk me down the aisle. All my doctor friends from Boston made the trip in the dead of winter. Some of my septuagenarian patients came, too. The church was full, standing room only for the ecumenical service. As you might have guessed, just about everybody on the island is a friend of Matt's.

He was incredibly handsome in a jazzy black tux, with his hair trimmed for the occasion, but not too short, his eyes bright and shining, his beautiful smile more radiant than it had ever been.

Can you see it, Nicky — with the snow lightly blowing in from the ocean? It was glorious.

"Are you as happy as I am?" Matt leaned toward me and whispered as we stood before the altar. "You look incredibly beautiful."

I felt myself blush, which was unlike me. Dr. Control, Dr. Self-Confidence, Dr. Hold It Together. But a feeling of unguarded vulnerability washed over me as I looked into Matt's eyes. This was so right.

"I've never been happier, never surer of anything in my life," I said.

We made our pledge on December 31, just before the New Year arrived. There was something almost magical about becoming husband and wife on New Year's Eve. It felt to me as if the whole world were celebrating with us.

Seconds after Matt and I pledged our vows, everyone in the church stood and yelled, "Happy New Year, Matt and Suzanne!"

Silvery white feathers were released from dozens of satin pouches that had been carefully strung from the ceiling. Matt and I were in a blizzard of angels and clouds and doves. We kissed and held each other tightly.

"How do you like the first moment of marriage, Mrs. Harrison?" he asked me. I think he liked saying, "Mrs. Harrison," and I liked hearing it for the first time.

"If I had known how wonderful it was going to be, I'd have insisted we marry twenty years ago," I said.

Matt grinned and went along with me.

"How could we? We didn't know each other."

"Oh, Matt," I said, "we've known each other all our lives. We must have."

I couldn't help remembering what Matt had said the night he proposed on the beach in front of my house. "Isn't it lucky," he'd said, "Suzanne didn't die in Boston and we have today to be together." I was *incredibly* lucky, and it gave me a chill as I stood there with Matt on our wedding night.

That's what it felt like — that was the exact feeling — and I'm so happy that now you were there.

Nicholas,

Matt and I went on a whirlwind, three-week honeymoon that started on New Year's Day.

The first week we were on Lanai in Hawaii. It is a glorious spot, the best, with only two hotels on the entire island. No wonder Bill Gates chose it for his honeymoon, too. I soon discovered that I loved Matt even more than I had before he proposed. We never wanted to leave Lanai. He would paint houses and finish his first collection of poems. I would be an island doctor.

The second week we went to Hana on Maui, and it was almost as special as Lanai. We had our mantra: *Isn't it lucky?* We must have said it a hundred times.

Matt and I spent the third week back home on the Vineyard, but we didn't see much of anyone, not even Jean or Melanie Bone and her kids. We were luxuriating in the newness and specialness of being together for the rest of our lives.

I suppose that not all honeymoons work out so well, but ours did. Nick, here's something your father did, something so thoughtful and special that I will always hold it close to my heart.

Every single day of our honeymoon, Matt woke me in bed — with a honeymoon present. Some of them were small, some were funny jokes, and some were extravagant, but every present came straight from Matt's heart.

Isn't it lucky?

I'll never forget this. It hit me like a wave of seasickness. Unfortunately, Matt had already gone to work and I was alone in the house. I sat down on the edge of the tub, feeling as if my life were draining away.

A cold sweat broke out on the back of my neck, and for the first time in over a year, I wanted to call a doctor. It seemed odd to want a second opinion. I was always diagnosing myself.

But today I felt just bad enough to want to ask someone else, "Hey what do you think?" Instead, I threw cold water on my face and told myself it was probably a touch of the flu, which was making the rounds. I hadn't been feeling well lately.

I took something to settle my stomach, dressed, and went to work. By noon I was feeling much better, and by dinner I had forgotten about it.

It wasn't until the next morning that I found myself sitting on the edge of the tub once more

— spent, tired, and feeling nauseated.

That's when I knew.

I called Matt on the cell phone, and he was surprised to hear from me so soon after he'd left the house.

"Are you okay? Is everything all right, Suzanne?"

"I think . . . that everything just got perfect," I told him. "If you can, I'd like you to come home right now. On your way could you stop at the drugstore? Would you pick up an EPT kit? I want to be absolutely sure, but, Matt, we're pregnant."

Nicholas,

You were growing inside me.

What can I tell you, Nicky — happiness flooded our hearts and every room of the beach cottage. It came like high tide on a full moon.

After the wedding, Matt had moved into my house. It was his idea. He said it was best to rent his place out since I was so established with my patients, and my proximity to the hospital was ideal. It was considerate and sweet of him, which is his way. For a big, tough guy, he's awfully nice. Your daddy *is* the best.

I would have missed the ocean, our sweet and salty garden, and the summer shutters that clack all night against the house when it's windy. But now I don't have to.

We decided to make the sunroom of the house yours. We thought you'd love the way the morning light comes pouring over the sills to fill every nook and cranny. Daddy and I began converting it into a perfect nursery, gathering things that we thought you might love.

We hung wallpaper that danced with Mother Goose stories. There were your bears, your first books, and colorful wall quilts that hung over your crib, the same crib Daddy had when he was a baby. Grandma Jean had saved it all these years. *Just for you, pumpkin.*

We jammed the shelves with far too many variously colored stuffed animals, and every variety of ball known to sportsmen.

Daddy made an oak rocking horse that boasted a beautiful one-of-a-kind crimson and gold mane. Daddy also made you delicately balanced mobiles filled with moons-and-stars galaxies. And a music box to hang in your crib.

Every time you pull the cord, it plays "Whistle a Happy Tune." Whenever I hear that song, I think of you.

We can't wait to meet you.

Nick,

Matt is at it again. A present was on the kitchen table when I got home from work. Gold paper covered in hearts and tied with blue ribbon concealed the contents. I couldn't possibly love him any more than I do.

I shook the small package, and a tiny note dropped out from under the bow.

It read, "Working late tonight, Suze, but thinking about you as always. Open this when you get in and get relaxed. I'll be back by ten. Matt."

I wondered where Matt was working until ten, but I let it go. I unwrapped the box carefully and lifted the tiny lid.

Inside was the most beautiful antique necklace. A sapphire locket in the shape of a heart hung from a silver chain. It was probably a hundred and fifty years old.

I pressed the clasp, and the heart opened

154

to reveal a message that had been engraved inside.

Nicholas, Suzanne, and Matt — Forever One.

Nick —

A few years back there was a book called *The Bridges of Madison County*. Its huge success was partly due to the fact that so many people seem to be missing romance and emotion in their lives. But an underlying premise of the novel was that romance can last for only a short time; in this particular book, only a couple of days for the main characters, Robert and Francesca. Romeo and Juliet were also star-crossed lovers whose love for each other ended tragically.

Nicky, please don't believe it. Love between two people can last a long time if the people love themselves some and are ready to give love to another person.

I was ready, and so was Matt.

Your father is starting to embarrass me. He is *too* good to me and makes me so happy. Like today. He did it to me again.

The house was filled with friends and

family when I came downstairs this morning, in floppy pink pajamas no less, with a sleepy expression on my face.

I had almost forgotten that today was my birthday. My thirty-sixth.

Matt hadn't. He had made a surprise breakfast . . . and I was surprised, all right. Unbelievably surprised.

"Matt?" I said, laughing, embarrassed, wrapping my arms around my wrinkled pajamas. "I'm going to murder you."

He weaved through the people crowded into the kitchen. He was holding a glass of orange juice for me and wearing a silly grin. "You're all witnesses. You heard my wife. She looks kind of harmless and sweet, but she's a killer. Happy birthday, Suzanne."

Grandma Jean handed me her present, and she insisted I open it then and there. Inside was a beautiful blue silk robe, which I put on to hide my flannels. I gave Jean a big hug for bringing the perfect gift.

"The grub is hot, pretty good, and it's *ready!*" Matt yelled, and everyone moved toward the groaning table, which was filled with eggs, several varieties of breakfast meats, sweet rolls, Jean's homemade babka, plenty of hot coffee.

After everyone had their fill of the sumptuous breakfast — and, yes, *birthday cake* —

they filed from the house and left us alone. Matt and I collapsed onto the big, comfy couch in the living room.

"So, how does it feel, Suzie? Another birthday?"

I couldn't help smiling. "You know how most people dread a birthday. They think, *Oh God, people will start looking at me like I'm old*. Well, I feel the exact opposite. I feel that every day is an extraordinary gift. Just to be here, and especially to be with you. Thanks for the birthday party. I love you."

Then Matt knew just the right thing to do. First, he leaned in and gave me the sweetest kiss on the lips. Then he carried me upstairs to our room, where we spent the rest of my birthday morning and, I must admit, most of my birthday afternoon.

Dear Nicky,

I am still a little shaky as I write about what happened a few weeks ago.

A local construction worker was rushed into the ER about eleven in the morning. Matt knew him and his family. The worker had fallen eighteen feet from a ladder and had suffered trauma to his head. Since I had previously been the attending physician on out-of-control nights at Mass. General, I had seen my share of trauma. I had the emergency room functioning on all cylinders, full tilt, snapping orders and directives.

The man's name was John Macdowell, thirty years old, married, with four kids. The MRI showed an epidermal hematoma. The pressure on his brain had to be alleviated immediately. Here was a young man, so close to dying, I thought. I didn't want to lose this young father.

I worked as hard as I have since I was in Boston.

It took nearly three hours to stabilize his condition. We almost lost him. He went into cardiac arrest. Finally, I knew we had him back. I wanted to kiss John Macdowell, just for being alive.

His wife came in with their children. She was weak with fear and couldn't stop tearing up every time she tried to speak. Her name was Meg, and she was carrying an infant boy. The poor young woman looked as if she were carrying the weight of the world on her shoulders. She probably felt that she *was* on this particular day.

I ordered a mild sedative for Mrs. Macdowell and sat with her until she could gather herself. The kids were obviously scared, too.

I took the second smallest, two years old, into my lap and gently stroked her hair. "Daddy is going to be okay," I said to the little girl.

The mother looked on, letting my words seep in. This was meant for her even more than for the children.

"He just fell down. Like you do sometimes. So we gave him medicine and a big bandage. He's going to be fine now. I'm his doctor, and I promise."

The little girl — all of the Macdowell kids — fastened on to every word I had to say. So did their mother.

"Thank you, Doctor," she finally whispered. "We love John so much. He's one of the good guys."

"I know he is. I could tell by the concern everybody showed. His entire crew came to the ER. We're going to keep John here for a few days. When it's time for him to leave, I'll tell you exactly what you'll need to do at home. He's stable now. Why don't I watch the kids. You can go in and see him."

The little girl climbed down from my lap. Mrs. Macdowell unraveled the baby from her arms and lowered him into mine. He was so tiny, probably only two or three months old. I doubted that his mother was more than twenty-five.

"Are you sure, Dr. Bedford? You can spare the time?" she asked me.

"I have all the time in the world for you, John, and the kids."

I sat there, holding the baby boy, and I couldn't help thinking about the little boy growing inside me. And also about mortality, and how we face it every day of our lives.

I already knew I was a pretty good doctor. But it was only at that moment, when I held the little Macdowell baby, that I knew I was going to be a good mother.

No, Nick, I knew I was going to be a *great* mom.

"What was *that?*" I said. "Matt? Honey?"

I spoke with difficulty. "Matt . . . something's going on. I'm in . . . some pain. *Whew.* There's more than a little pain, actually."

I dropped my fork on the floor of the Black Dog Tavern, where we were having dinner. *This couldn't be happening. Not yet.* I was still weeks away from my delivery date. There was no way I could be having a contraction.

Matt jumped into action. He was more prepared for the moment than I was. He tossed cash onto the table and escorted me out of the Black Dog.

Part of me knew what was happening. Or so I believed. *Braxton Hicks.* Contractions that don't represent true labor. Women sometimes have these pains, occasionally even in their first trimester, but when they come in the third, they can be mistaken for actual labor.

However, my pain seemed to be *above* my uterus, spreading up and under my left lung. It came like a sharp knife. Literally took my breath away.

We got into the Jeep and headed directly to the hospital.

"I'm sure it's nothing," I said. "Nicky's just giving a heads-up, letting us know he's physically fit."

"Good," Matt said, but he kept driving.

I had been getting weekly monitoring because this was considered a high-risk pregnancy. But everything had been fine, even a joy, up until now. If I were in trouble, I would have known it. Wouldn't I? I was always on the lookout for the least little problem. The fact that I'm a doctor made me even more prepared.

I was wrong. I was in trouble. The kind of trouble you're not quite sure you want to know about before it happens.

This is the story of how we both almost died.

Nicholas,

We had the best doctor on Martha's Vineyard, and one of the best in all of New England. Dr. Constance Cotter arrived at the hospital about ten minutes after I got there with Matt.

I felt fine by then, but Connie monitored me herself for the next two hours. I could see her urgency; I could read it in the tightness of her jaw. She was worrying about my heart. Was it strong enough? She was worrying about you, Nicky.

"This is potentially dangerous," Connie said, sparing me no illusions. "Suzanne, your pressure is so high that part of me wants to start labor right now. I know it's not time, but you've got me worried. What I *am* going to do is keep you here tonight. And as many nights as I feel are warranted. No, you have no say in this."

I looked at Connie like, You must be kidding. I was a doctor. I lived right down the road from the hospital. I would come in immediately if necessary.

"Don't even think about it. You're staying. Check in, and I'll be up to see you before I go. This isn't negotiable, Suzanne."

It was strange to be checking in to the hospital where I worked. An hour or so later, Matt and I sat in my room waiting for Connie to return. I was telling him what I knew so far, in particular about a condition called preeclampsia.

"What exactly is preeclampsia, Suzanne?" he asked. He wanted every detail explained in clear layman's terms. He was asking all the right questions. So I told him, and he shifted uncomfortably in his chair.

"You wanted to know," I said.

Connie finally came in. She took my blood pressure again. "Suzanne," she said, "it's higher than it was. If it doesn't go down in the next few hours, I'm inducing labor."

I had never seen Matt look, or act, so nervous. "I'm going to stay here with you tonight, Suzanne," he said.

"Don't be silly," I told him. "Sit in an uncomfortable chair and watch me sleep? That's crazy."

But Connie looked at me and, in the clinical tone that she uses only for patients, said,

"I think that's a very good idea. Matt should stay with you, Suzanne."

Then Connie checked my pressure once more before leaving for the night.

I studied her face, looking for any kind of sign of trouble. *What kind of look was that?*

Connie stared at me oddly and I couldn't quite figure it out.

Then she said, "Suzanne, I'm not getting a strong reading from the baby's heart. The baby has to come out *now*."

Dear Nicholas,

All my life I had wanted a baby. I wanted to experience natural childbirth, just as my mother and grandmother had. Connie knew how important a natural delivery was to me. Matt and I had attended Lamaze classes together. She'd heard me go on and on about it in her office, and even over lunch.

I could see the sadness and pain in her face when she leaned over to me. She grasped my hand tightly in both of hers.

"Suzanne," she whispered, "I wanted to bring this baby into the world the way you hoped it would happen. But you know I'm not going to put either you or this baby at risk. We have to do a c-section."

Tears welled up in my eyes, but I nodded. "I know, Connie. I trust you."

Everything began to move too fast after that.

Connie inserted an IV in my arm and administered magnesium sulfate. I immediately felt sicker than ever. A blinding headache overcame me.

Matt was right there as they prepped me for the c-section. He was told by a new attending doctor that this was an emergency. He couldn't stay with me.

Thank God, Connie came back in just then and overrode the decision.

Connie then told me what was happening.

My liver was swollen. The blood platelet count was alarming, and my blood pressure was 190/130.

Worse, Nicky, *your* heartbeat was weakening.

"You're going to be okay, Suzanne," I kept hearing Connie say. Her voice was like an echo from a distant canyon. The room lights above my head appeared to be spinning out of control.

"What about Nicky?" I whispered through parched lips.

I waited for her to say, "And Nicky will be fine, too."

But Connie didn't say it, and tears came to my eyes again.

I was rolled into the operating room, where they were not only ready to deliver a baby but also to transfuse me with eight units of blood. My platelet count had dropped. I knew what was going on here. If I started bleeding internally I would die.

As I was being given the epidural anesthesia, I saw Dr. Leon, my cardiologist, standing right by the anesthetist. *Why was Leon here? Oh God, no. Please don't do this. Oh please, please, please. I beg you.* An oxygen mask was placed over my face. I tried to resist.

Connie raised her voice. "No, Suzanne. Take the oxygen."

I felt as if I were on fire. I wasn't able to logically attribute it to the magnesium sulfate. I didn't know that my kidneys were shutting down, my platelets were dangerously low, my blood pressure had risen even more, to an alarming 200/115. I didn't know that steroid injections were being administered to optimize the baby's lung function and his prospect of survival.

The next few minutes were a blur. I saw a retractor come out. There were concerned looks from Connie, and then evasive eye contact.

I heard staccato orders and cold, unfeeling machine beeps and Matt chanting only positive things. I heard a loud sucking noise as amniotic fluid and blood were cleaned out of me.

There was numbness, some dizziness, and the oddest feeling of not being there, of not being anywhere, actually.

What brought me out of my surreal feeling of having entered another world was *a cry*. A distinct and mighty cry. You had announced your arrival like a strong warrior.

I began to cry, and so did Matt and Connie. You were such a little thing, just over six pounds. But so strong. And alert. Especially considering the stress you had been through.

You looked right at Daddy and me. I'll never forget it. *The first time ever I saw your face.*

I got to hold you in my arms before you were whisked away to the NICU. I got to look into the beautiful eyes that you struggled to keep open, and I got to whisper for the first time, "I love you."

Nicholas the Warrior!

Katie

Fear and confusion swept over Katie again that night. While she read a few more diary pages, she forced herself to eat pasta primavera and drink tea. It didn't help.

Everything was moving way too fast in her head, and especially inside her sore, bloated body.

A baby boy had been born. Nicholas the Warrior.

Another child was growing inside her.

Katie had to think and be logical about this. What were all the possibilities? What could really be happening now?

Matt had been cheating on Suzanne all of these months?

Matt had been cheating and I wasn't the first?

Matt had left Suzanne and Nicholas for some reason that was yet to be revealed in the diary? They were divorced?

Suzanne had left Matt for somebody else?

Suzanne had died — her heart had finally given out?

Suzanne was alive, but very ill?

Where was Suzanne right now? Maybe she should try to call her on Martha's Vineyard. Maybe they should talk. Katie wasn't sure if that was a good idea or if it would be one of her worst blunders ever.

She tried to work it through. What did she have to lose? A little pride, but not much else. *But what about Suzanne?* What if she had no idea about Matt? Was that even faintly possible? Of course it was. Wasn't that pretty much what had happened to Katie? Anything seemed possible to her right now. Anything *was* possible. So what had really happened?

This was so overwhelming — unbearable. The man she had loved, and trusted, and thought she completely understood, had left her. Wasn't that just typical these days? Wasn't it sad?

She remembered a particular moment with Matt that kept her going. He had woken up beside her one night and was crying. She had held Matt in her arms for a long time. She stroked his cheek. Finally Matt had whispered, "I'm trying hard to get everything behind me. I will. I promise, Katie."

God, this was crazy!

Katie pounded her thigh with a closed

fist. Her pulse was racing too fast. Her breasts really hurt.

She pushed herself out of her sofa, hurried into the bathroom, and threw up the pasta she'd just eaten.

A little while later, Katie went into the kitchen and fixed herself more tea. She and Guinevere sat staring at the four walls. She had hung the kitchen cabinets herself. The guys at Chinatown Lumber knew her all too well. She had her own toolbox and prided herself on never having to call the super to fix anything. *So fix what's wrong with your heart,* Katie thought. *Fix that!*

Finally, she reached for the phone.

Merlin opened one sleepy eye as she nervously punched some numbers and heard a pickup on the other end of the line.

"Hi, Mom. It's me," she said in a voice that came out much smaller than she intended.

"I know, Katie. What's the matter, sweetheart? Couldn't you just come home for a couple of days? I think it would do us all a world of good."

This was so hard, so bad.

"Could you get Daddy to pick up, too?"

she asked. "Get Daddy, please."

"I'm here, Katie," her father said. "I'm on in the den. I picked up when the phone rang. How are you?"

She sighed loudly. "Well . . . I'm pregnant," Katie finally said.

Then all three of them were crying over the phone — because that's the way they were. But Katie's mother and father were already comforting her, saying, "It's all right, Katie, we love you, we're with you, we understand."

Because that's the way they were, too.

The Diary

Nicholas,

Just for the record. You started sleeping through the night early on. Not every night, but most, starting when you were about two weeks old, to the envy of all the other moms!

When you go through your little growth spurts, you wake up hungry. And what a little eater you are! You will eat *anything* — whether you're breast-fed, or bottle-fed formula, or water, you chow down and aren't picky.

On your first visit to the pediatrician after the initial hospital checkups, the doctor couldn't believe how you were already focusing on the toys she had laid out. She exclaimed, "He's extraordinary — sensational, Suzanne." And she said you're "so smart and so strong" because when she turned you on your tummy you lifted your head.

That's a great feat for a two-week-old. Nicholas the Warrior!

You were baptized at the Church of Mary Magdalene. It was a beautiful day. You wore my christening gown — a handmade heirloom of my aunt Romelle's family in Newburgh, New York. It was also worn by my cousins and various other relatives over the past fifty years, and it was in perfect condition. You looked sweet and were such a charmer.

Monsignor Dwyer was completely taken with you. During the baptism, you kept reaching for the service book and touching his hand. You were looking right at him, attentive as could be.

Toward the end of the service, after you hadn't missed a trick, Monsignor Dwyer said to you, "I don't know *what* you're going to be when you grow up, Nicholas. On second thought — you *are* grown up."

It's my first day back at work today. Not surprisingly, I miss you already. No, let me make that a little stronger: *I'm bereft without you.*

I wrote something as I sat thinking about you — even between patients.

> Nickels and dimes
> I love you in rhythms
> I love you in rhymes
> I love you in laughter
> Here and ever after
> Then I love you a million
> Gazillion more times!

I think I could come up with dozens of Nicky nursery rhymes if I tried. They just come to me when you do something silly, or smile, or even when you sleep. What can I say? You inspire poetry.

Matt loves them, too. And coming from him, it's a real compliment. Make no mistake about it, your daddy is definitely the writer in this family. But I still love writing these little love poems to you.

Yikes, here comes one now!

You're my little Nicky Knack
I love you so, you love me back.
I love your toes, your knees, your nose,
And everywhere a big kiss goes.
I kiss you tons, and know what then?
I have to kiss you once again.

Okay, little man, I have to go now. My next patient is here already. If she knew what I was doing behind closed doors in my office, the poor woman would flee to the free clinic in Edgartown.

I thought I'd ease into work with a half day just to get used to the routine again. But ever since I arrived this morning, all I wanted to do was look at your pictures and write silly poems.

Anyone peeking in at me would think I was in love.

I am.

Nicky, it's me again —

I heard you crying tonight and got up to see what was the matter. You looked up at me with such sad little eyes. Your eyes are so blue, and always so expressive.

I looked to see if you needed changing — but it wasn't that. Then I checked to see if you were hungry — but it wasn't that, either.

So I lifted you up and sat with you in the rocker next to your crib.

Back and forth we went, back and forth, in a rhythm about double the rush of the ocean surf.

Your eyes started slowly closing, and your tears dissolved into sweet dreams. I placed you back in your crib and watched your heart-shaped bottom rising in the air. Then I turned you over on your back and watched your little tummy rise and fall.

I think all you wanted was a little company. Could you really just have wanted to be rocked and held and talked to?

I'm here, sweetie. I'm right here, and I'm not going anywhere. I'll always be right here.

"What are you doing, Suzie?" Matt whispered. I hadn't heard him come into the nursery. Daddy can be as quiet as a cat.

"Nick couldn't sleep."

Matt looked into the crib and saw your tiny hand clenched to your mouth like a teething ring.

"God, he's beautiful," Matt whispered. "I mean it — he is gorgeous."

I looked down at you. There wasn't an inch of you that didn't make my heart leap.

Matt put his arms around my waist. "Want to dance, Mrs. Harrison?" He hadn't called me that since our wedding day. My heart fluttered like a sparrow in a birdbath.

"I think they're playing our song."

And to the high, plucky notes that came squeaking out of your music box, Matt and I danced round and round in your nursery that night. Past the stuffed animals, past Mother Goose and your homemade rocking horse, past the stars and the moons that float from your homemade mobile. We danced slowly and lovingly in the low light of your tiny cocoon.

When the music finally wound down to its

final note, Matt kissed me and said, "Thank you, Suzanne. Thank you for this night, this dance, and most of all for this little boy. My whole world is right here, in this room. If I never had another thing, I would have everything."

And then strangely — magically — as if your music box were just taking a rest, it played one more sweet refrain.

Nick,

Melanie Bone came over to baby-sit while I went to work. Full day, full load. Melanie's kids were in Maine with her mother for a week, so she gave Grandma Jean a breather. It feels strange to leave you for this long, and I can't stop thinking about what you're doing now.

And *now.*

And *now.*

The last time I felt this tired, I was working my butt off at Mass. General in Boston. Maybe it's because I'm juggling so many things again these days. Having a job and a baby is even harder than I thought. My respect for all mothers has never been higher, and it was high to begin with. Working mothers, mothers who stay at home, single mothers — they are all so amazing.

Something happened at the hospital today that made me think of your delivery.

A forty-one-year-old woman who was on vacation from New York was brought in. She was in her seventh month, and not doing well. Then all hell broke loose in the emergency room. She began to hemorrhage. It was so terrible. The poor woman ended up losing her baby, and I had to try to console her.

You probably wonder why I'm writing about this. Even I thought twice before sharing this sad story with you.

But it has made me realize more than ever how vulnerable we are, how life can be like walking on a high wire. Falling seems a tiny misstep away. Just seeing that poor woman today, and remembering how lucky we were, made me catch my breath.

Oh, Nicky, sometimes I wish I could hide you like a precious heirloom. But what is life if you don't live it? I think I know that as well as anyone.

There's a saying I remember from my grandmother: One today is worth two tomorrows.

Dear Show-off,

You are starting to hold your own bottle. No one can believe it. This little guy feeding himself at two months. Every new experience that you have, I take as a gift to me and Daddy.

Sometimes I can be such a goofball. Reduced to gauzy visions of station wagons, suburbia, and bronzed baby shoes. So I had to do it. I had to have your picture professionally taken.

Every mother has to do it once. Right?

Today is the perfect day. Daddy is off on a trip to New York, where someone has taken a liking to his poems. He's very low-key about it, but it's the greatest news. So the two of us are home alone. I have a plan.

I got you dressed in washed-out blue overalls (so cool), your little work boots (just like Daddy's), and a Red Sox baseball cap (with the peak bent just so).

The cap had to go! You freaked out over it; I guess you thought I was trying to attach antlers to your head.

Here's the whole scene, just in case you don't remember it.

When we got to the You Oughta Be in Pictures photography studio, you looked at me as if to say, *Surely you have made a grotesque mistake.*

Maybe I had.

The photographer was a fifty-year-old man who had no kidside manner at all. It wasn't that he was mean, he was just clueless. I got the idea that his real specialty might be still life, because he tried to warm you up with a variety of fruits and vegetables.

Well, one thing is certain. We now have a unique set of pictures. You begin with the surprised look, which quickly dissolves into a slightly more annoyed attitude. After that you enter the cantankerous phase, which swiftly disintegrates into the angry portion of our program. And last but not least, irreconcilable meltdown.

There is a small consolation. At least you can't tell Daddy. He'd get too much mileage out of his *I told you so*s.

Forgive me this one. I promise I will never show these pictures to new girlfriends, old fraternity brothers, or Grandma Jean. She'd have them in every shop window on the Vineyard before dusk.

Nicky,

It was a little cool out, but I bundled you up and we took a picnic basket down to Bend in the Road Beach — to celebrate Daddy's thirty-seventh birthday. *God, he's old!*

We made castles and sand angels and wrote your name in big bold letters until the surf came and washed it away.

Then we *wrote it again,* high enough up so the water couldn't reach it.

It was such a total blast to watch you and Daddy play together. You are very much a chip off the old block, two peas in a pod, Laurel and Hardy! Your mannerisms, your ways, your gestures, are Matt's. And vice versa. Sometimes when I look at you, I can imagine Daddy when he was a boy. You are both joyful, graceful, and athletic, beautiful to watch.

So there you are, just back to our blanket from fighting sand monsters and friendly sea urchins, when Matt reaches into his pocket and pulls out a letter. He hands it to me.

"The publisher in New York didn't want my collection — *yet* — but here's a consolation prize."

He had sent a poem off to a magazine called the *Atlantic Monthly*. They accepted it. He didn't even tell me he was doing it. Said he didn't want it to be out there just in case it didn't happen. But it did, Nicky, and he got the letter on his birthday.

I asked if I could read it, and Matt unfolded a separate sheet of paper. It was the poem, and he had it with him all this time.

My eyes teared up when I saw the title, "Nicholas and Suzanne."

Matt told me that he had been writing down all the things I say and sing to you, that he'd strain to overhear my little poems and rock-a-bye rhymes.

He said that this wasn't just his poem but mine, too. He told me that it was *my voice* he heard in these lines; so we had created it together.

Daddy read part of it out loud, above the crashing surf and screeching gulls.

Nicholas and Suzanne

Who makes the treetops wave their hands?

196

And draws home ships from foreign lands,
And spins plain straw back into gold
And has a love too large to hold . . .

Who chases the rain from the sky?
And sings the moon a lullaby,
And grants the wishes from a well
And hears whole songs sung from a shell . . .

Who has the gift of making much?
From everything they hold or touch,
Who turns pure joy back into life?
For this I thank my son, my wife.

What could be better than this?
Absolutely nothing.
Daddy said this was his best birthday ever.

Nicholas,

Something unexpected has happened, and I'm afraid it's not so good.

It was time again for your dreaded baby shots. I hated to have to put you through it. Your pediatrician on the Vineyard was on vacation, so I decided to call a doctor friend in Boston. It was time for a visit to Beantown, anyway.

While I was in Boston, I would get my own physical. It was also a chance to catch up with friends, maybe do a little window shopping on Newbury Street, eat at Harvard Gardens, and, best of all, show you off, Nicky Mouse.

We took the ferry over to Woods Hole and hit Route 3 by nine in the morning. This was our first adventure off the island. *Nicholas's Trip to the Big City!*

Your appointment was first. The children's office looked exactly as it always had.

Highlights, crayons, and blocks lay every-where. A black clock cat moved its tail and eyes back and forth to the time. You were fixated on it.

Other babies were crying and fidgety, but you sat there as quiet as a little mouse, checking out these new surroundings.

"Nicholas Harrison," the receptionist finally called.

It was funny to hear your name announced so officially by a complete stranger. I almost expected you to answer, "Present."

It was good to see my old buddy Dan Anderson, and he couldn't believe how big you were already. He said he saw a lot of me in you, and of course that thrilled me. But in fairness I had to show him pictures of Daddy, too.

"You seem so happy, Suzanne," Dan said as he measured, tapped, and tuned you up, Nicky.

"I am, Dan. Never been happier. It's great."

"Leaving the big city did you a world of good. And just look at this future quarterback you've got here."

I beamed. "He is the best little boy on this earth. Like you've never heard that before. Right?"

"Not from you, Suzanne." He handed you

back over to me. "It's wonderful seeing you again, Mother Bedford. And as far as this one goes, he's the poster child for good health."

Of course, I already knew that.

Now it was my turn.

I sat at the edge of the examining-room table, already dressed, waiting for my doctor, Dr. "Philadelphia" Phil Berman, to come back in. Phil had been my doctor in Boston and had kept in touch with the specialist on Martha's Vineyard. They complemented each other nicely.

The physical had taken a little longer than usual. One of the nurses outside was watching over you, but I was anxious for a hug and also to hit the road back to the Vineyard. That's when Phil came in and asked me to step into his office.

We were old friends, so we exchanged small talk for a minute or two. Then Phil got down to business.

"Your stress test doesn't look too good to me, Suzanne. I noticed a few irregularities on your EKG. I took the liberty of calling downstairs to Dr. Davis. I know Gail was your cardiologist when you were here as a patient. She has your records from the island. She's going to squeeze you in today."

"Wait a minute, Phil," I said. I was stunned. This had to be wrong. I was feeling fine — *great,* actually. I was in the best shape of my life. "That can't be right. Are you sure?"

"I know your history, and I would be remiss in not insisting that Gail Davis take a look. Hey, Suzanne, you're here already. Martha's Vineyard is a long way off. Just do it. It won't take long. We'll keep Nicholas here until you're done. Our pleasure."

And then Phil continued, his tone changing ever so slightly, "Suzanne, you and I have known each other for a long time. I just want you to take care of whatever this might be. It could be absolutely nothing, but I want a second opinion. You'd give the same advice to any of your own patients."

It felt like déjà vu, walking through the halls, heading to Gail Davis's office. *Dear God, please don't let this happen again. Not now. Oh please, God. Everything in my life is so good.*

I entered the waiting room as if I were walking in a misty fog in a bad dream. I couldn't focus or think.

The ominous mantra that kept repeating loudly in my brain was *Tell me this isn't happening.*

A nurse walked right up to me. Actually, I knew her from the hospital visits after my heart attack. "Suzanne, you can come with me now."

I followed her like a prisoner about to be executed.

Tell me this isn't happening.

I was in there for nearly two hours. I think I was given every cardiology test known. I was worried about you, even though I knew you were in good hands at Dr. Berman's office.

When it was finally over, Gail Davis came in. She looked grave but Gail usually does, even at parties where I've seen her socially. I reminded myself of that, but it didn't really help.

"You have *not* had another heart attack, Suzanne. Let me put your mind at ease about that. But what I detect is some weakness in *two* of your valves. I suspect it was caused by the last cardiac infarction. Or possibly the pregnancy.

"Because the valves are damaged, your heart is having some difficulty pumping blood. You know where I'm going, Suzanne, but I feel compelled to alert you. This is a warning, a very lucky warning."

"I don't feel very lucky," I said.

"Some people never get a warning, and so

they don't get a chance to fix what could be about to break. When you get back to Martha's Vineyard, there'll be more tests, then we can talk about your options. Valves may have to be replaced, or possibly not."

Now I was having trouble catching my breath. I absolutely refused to cry in front of Gail. "It's so strange," I said. "Everything can be going along just great, and then one day, *whack,* you're blind-sided — a lousy, crummy blow you didn't see coming."

Gail Davis didn't say anything; she just put her hand gently on my back.

Nicky,

In the words of a feisty little Italian girl, Michele Lentini, who used to be my best friend back in Cornwall, New York, *oh, marone.*

Or, in the words of the Blues Brothers, *They're not going to catch us, we're on a mission from God!*

I watched you in the rearview mirror, your little feet kicking up and down, your arms reaching toward me. The world swept past us on both sides, and it felt to me that we were falling home instead of just going there.

I talked to you, Nicky, really talked.

"My life feels so connected to you. It seems impossible that something bad could happen to me now. But I guess that's just the false sense of security that love gives."

I thought about that for a second. Falling in love with Matt, and being so much in love with him now, *had* given me a feeling of security.

How could anything harm us? How could anything really bad happen?

And you give me this same sense, Nick. How could anything happen to break us apart? How could I *not* see you grow up? That would be too cruel for God to let happen.

The tears I had held back in Dr. Davis's office suddenly flooded my eyes. I quickly wiped them away. I concentrated on the road home and kept our journey at my usual slow and steady pace.

I talked to you in the little rearview mirror I have that looks directly at your car seat. "So let's make a plan. All right, baby boy? Every time I can make you smile means that we have one more year together, a whole year for every smile. Magical thinking, Nicky, that's what this is. Already we have a dozen more years together, because you've smiled at least that many times on this car ride. At this rate, I'll be a hundred and thirty-six, you a spry eighty-two."

I started to laugh at my own crazy humor.

Suddenly you broke into the biggest smile I have ever seen you make. You made me laugh so hard, I just looked back and whispered, "Nicholas, Suzanne, and Matt — Forever One."

That is my prayer.

Nicholas,

Four long, nervous weeks have passed since I received the troubling news in Boston. Matt is out with you riding in the Jeep, and I'm sitting in the kitchen with the sun falling through the window like yellow streamers in a parade. It's so beautiful.

The medical opinions are all in. I have heart-valve disease, but it is treatable. For the moment, we won't be replacing the valves, and we definitely won't be considering a heart transplant. Everything will be treated with radiation for now.

I have been warned, though: *Life doesn't go on forever. Enjoy every moment of it.*

I can smell the morning unfolding, carrying with it the song and salt and the grassy perfume of the marshes.

My eyes are closed, and the wind chimes are being tickled by the ocean breeze outside the window.

"Isn't it lucky?" I finally say out loud.

"That I'm sitting here, looking out on this beautiful day. . . .

"That I live on Martha's Vineyard, so close to the ocean that I could throw a stone into the surf — if I were the kind of person who could throw stones far. . . .

"That I am a doctor and love what I do. . . .

"That somehow, however improbable, I found Matthew Harrison and we fell wildly in love. . . .

"That we have a little boy with the most beautiful blue eyes, and the most wonderful smile, and the nicest disposition, and a baby smell I just love.

"Isn't it lucky, Nicky? Isn't it just so lucky?"

That's what I think, anyway.

That's another of my prayers.

Nicholas,

You are growing up before our eyes, and it is such a glorious thing to watch. I *savor* each moment. I hope all the other mommies and daddies are remembering to savor these moments and have the time to do so.

You love to ride bikes with Mommy. You have your own little Boston Bruins helmet and a seat that holds you snuggly and safely on the back of my bike. I tie a water bottle with a ribbon and attach it to your seat for you to enjoy on the ride — and we're off.

You love singing, and looking at all the people and sights on the Vineyard. Fun for Mama, too.

You have a lot of the blondest of blond curls. I know that if I cut them, they'll be gone forever. You'll really be a little boy then, no longer a baby.

I love watching you grow, but at the same time I don't like seeing this time fly by so fast. It's hard to explain; I don't really know how. But there's something so precious about watching your child day after day after day. I want to hold on to every moment, every smile, every single hug and kiss. I suppose it has to do with *loving* to be needed and *needing* to give love.

I want to relive this all over again.

Every single moment since you were born.

I told you I would be a great mom.

Each day lately has felt so complete for me.

Every morning, without fail, Matt turns to me before we get up. He kisses me, and then whispers in my ear, "We have today, Suzanne. Let's get up and see our boy."

But today feels a little different to me. I'm not exactly sure why, but my intuition tells me there's something going on. I don't know if I like it. I'm not quite sure yet.

After Daddy goes off to work and I have you fed and dressed, I still don't feel right.

It is an odd feeling. Not too bad, but definitely not too good. I am lightheaded, and more tired than usual.

So tired, in fact, I have to lie down.

I must have fallen asleep after I tucked you into your crib, because when I opened my eyes again, the church bells from the town were striking.

It was noon already. Half the day was gone.

That's when I decided to find out what was going on.

And now, I know.

Nicholas,

After Daddy put you to bed tonight, the two of us sat out on the porch and watched the sun set on the ocean in a blaze of streaking oranges and reds. He has the most amazing touch and was patiently stroking my arms and legs, which I love more than almost anything on the planet. I could let him do this for hours, and sometimes I do.

He is very excited about his poetry lately. His great dream is to have a collection published, and suddenly people are interested. I love the excitement in his voice, and I let him talk.

"Matthew, something happened today," I finally said, once he had told me all his news.

He turned on the couch and sat up straight. His eyes were full of worry, his brow creased.

"I'm sorry, I'm sorry." I soothed him. "Something good happened today."

I could feel Matt relax in my arms and also saw it on his face. "So what happened, Suzanne? Tell me all about your day."

The nice thing is that your daddy really wants to hear about these things. He listens, and even asks questions. Some men don't.

"Well, on Wednesdays I don't go to work unless there's an emergency. There wasn't any today, thank God. So I stayed home with Nick."

Matt put his head in my lap and let me stroke his thick, sandy brown hair. He likes this finger combing almost as much as I like his tickling. "That sounds pretty nice. Maybe I'll start taking Wednesdays off, too," he teased.

"Isn't it lucky," I said, "that I get to spend Wednesdays with Nicky?"

Matt pulled my face to his and we kissed. I don't know how long this incredible honeymoon of ours is going to last, but I love it and don't want it to end. Matthew is the best friend I could have ever wished for. Just about any woman would be lucky to have him. And if it ever, ever came to that — another mommy for you — I'm sure Matt would choose wisely.

"Is that what happened? You and Nick had a great day together?" he asked.

I looked deeply into Matt's eyes. "I'm

215

pregnant," I told him.

And then Matt did just the right thing: He kissed me gently. "I love you," he whispered. "Let's be careful, Suzanne."

"Okay," I whispered back. "I'll be very careful."

Nicholas,

I don't know why, but life is usually more complicated than the plans that we make. I visited my cardiologist on the Vineyard, told him about the pregnancy, had a few tests. Then, on his recommendation, I went to Boston to see Dr. Davis again.

I hadn't mentioned the checkup to Matt, thinking it might worry him. So I went to work for a few hours, then I drove to Boston in the afternoon. I promised myself that I would talk to Matt as soon as I got home.

The porch light of the house was on when I pulled into the driveway at about seven that night. I was late. Matt was already home. He had relieved Grandma Jean of her baby-sitting duties.

I could smell the delicious aroma of home cooking: chicken, pan potatoes, and gravy warming the whole house. *Oh, my God, he made dinner,* I thought.

"Where's Nicky?" I asked as I entered the kitchen.

"I put him to bed. He was exhausted. Long day for you, sweets. You're being careful?"

"Yeah," I said, kissing him on the cheek. "I actually only saw a couple of patients this morning. I had to go to Boston and see Dr. Davis."

Matt stopped stirring the gravy. He stared at me and didn't say another word. He looked so hurt that I couldn't stand it.

"I should have told you, Matthew. I didn't want to worry you. I *knew* you would, and I didn't want you to; I knew you'd want to come to Boston with me."

It was a nervous, run-on thought, my attempt to explain what I had done. It wasn't right, but it wasn't wrong, either. Matt decided to leave my decision at that.

"Well?" he said. "What did Dr. Davis have to say?"

My mind traced back to Gail Davis's office, back to the edge of the examining table, where I had sat so tenuously in a blur of emotions: *What did she say? What did she say?*

"Well, I told her about the baby."

"Right."

"And she was . . . she was very concerned. Gail wasn't pleased."

218

The next few words locked in my throat, nearly closed off my breathing. I almost couldn't speak. Tears flooded to my eyes, and I started to shake.

"She said it was too risky for me to be pregnant. She said I shouldn't have this baby."

Matt's eyes filled with tears now, too. He took a breath. Then he spoke, splitting the silence between us.

"Suzanne, I agree with her. I couldn't bear to risk losing you."

I was crying, sobbing terribly, still shaking badly. "Don't give up on this baby, Matt."

I looked at him, waiting for some comforting words. But he was too quiet. He finally shook his head slowly. "I'm sorry, Suzanne."

Suddenly I needed to breathe some fresh air, to escape, to be by myself. I left the house in a spin. I ran through the tall sea grass until I reached the beach. Shaken, winded, fatigued. There was a loud roaring noise in the space between my ears. It wasn't the sound of the ocean.

I lay down in the sand and wept. I felt awful, so inconsolably sad for the baby inside me. I thought about Matt and you waiting for me back at the house. Was I being selfish, headstrong, foolish? I was a doctor. I knew the risks.

This baby was a precious and unexpected gift. I couldn't give it up. I held myself and rocked with that feeling for what seemed like hours. I talked to the little baby growing inside me. Then I looked up at the full moon, and I knew it was time to go back to the house.

Matt was waiting for me in the kitchen. I saw him in the mellow, yellow light as I trudged up from the beach. I started to cry again.

I did a strange thing, then, and I'm not exactly sure why I knocked on the door, then knelt on the first step. Maybe I was tired and drained from the long, stressful day. Maybe it was something else, something more important, something I still can't explain.

Maybe I was remembering the English king who had knelt in the snow hoping not to be excommunicated, to be forgiven by Pope Gregory.

I had been hurting badly out on the beach, but I also knew I had acted selfishly. I shouldn't have run away and left you and Matt alone at the house.

"Forgive me for running off like that," I said as Matt opened the screen door. "For running away from you. I should have stayed and talked it out."

"You know better," he whispered, and gently stroked my hair. "There's nothing to forgive, Suzanne."

Matt pulled me to my feet and into his

arms. A feeling of relief swept through me. I listened to the strong beating of his heart. I let him snuggle the top of my head with his chin. I let his warmth seep into me.

"It's just that I want to keep this baby Matt. Is that so terrible?"

"No, Suzanne. That isn't terrible. It's losing you that I couldn't bear. If I lost you, I don't think I could live. I love you so much. I love you and Nicky."

Oh, Nicky,

Life can be unforgiving sometimes. Learn that lesson, sweet boy. I had just gotten home from a couple of hours at the office. Routine really, nothing unusual, nothing stressful. Actually, I was feeling pretty chipper.

I drove back to the cottage to take a catnap before seeing one more patient in the afternoon. You were at Grandma's house for the day. Matt had a job over in East Chop.

I was going to take it easy, catch a nice, healthy, restful snooze. I had an appointment to see Connie in town the next day — *about the baby.*

I fell onto the bed, feeling dizzy suddenly. My heart began to pound a little. Strange. I felt a headache coming on, out of nowhere.

It was about to rain buckets, and the barometric pressure had dropped. I sometimes get headaches when that happens.

My appointment with Connie was the next

day, but I was deliberating over whether I should wait until then. Maybe I would feel better in an hour, or when the rain finally came.

I was so nervous about staying healthy that I was driving myself into neurotic symptoms, for God's sake.

Easy, Suzanne, I told myself. *Lie down and close your eyes and tell every part of your body to relax.*

Your eyes, your mouth, your chest, your belly, your arms, your legs, your feet, your toes.

Relax them all and slip under the blanket, the Golden Fleece.

All you need is an hour, a break, and when you wake up, it will all feel better.

Just fall asleep, fall asleep now, fall . . .

"Suzanne, what's the matter?"

I turned over on the daybed at the sound of Matt's gentle whisper. I still didn't feel too good. He leaned in closer, and he looked concerned. "Suzanne? Can you talk, sweetheart?"

"Seeing Connie tomorrow," I finally said. This was strange. It took all my strength just to get those few words out.

"You're seeing Connie right now," Matt said.

When we arrived at Connie's office, she took one look at me and said, "No offense, but you look less than stellar, Suzanne."

She took my blood pressure, then blood and urine samples, and finally an EKG. All through the tests, I was in a daze. I felt hollow inside, and more than a little worried.

Following my examination, she sat down with Matt and me. Connie didn't look happy. "Your blood pressure is up, but it will be a day or so before we get your blood work back. I'll put a rush on it. In some ways things are steady, but I don't like how you were feeling today. Or how you *look*. I'm inches away from admitting you. I agree with Dr. Davis about the abortion. It's your decision, of course, but you're putting yourself at grave risk."

"God, Connie," I said, "short of stopping my practice altogether, I'm doing everything else right. I'm being so careful, so good."

"Then stop working altogether," she said without missing a beat. "I'm not kidding, Suzanne. I don't like what's going on with you. If you go home and make your *number one priority* absolute rest, then we have a chance. Otherwise, I'm checking you in."

I knew Connie meant what she said. She always did. "I'm going home now," I mumbled. "I can't give up on this baby."

Dear Nicholas,

I am so sorry, sweetie. A month has passed and you have kept me busy. I am also tired, and I haven't had a chance to write. I'll try to make it up to you.

At eleven months, your favorite words are *Dada, Mama, wow, watch, boat, ball, water* (*wa*), *car,* and your very favorite is *LIGHT.* You are crazy about lights. You say, "Yight."

You are like a windup toy these days. You just keep going and going and going and going and going.

I was in the middle of giving you my "be a good boy" rap when the phone rang. It was Connie Cotter's nurse, who put me on hold for the doctor.

It seemed to take forever before Connie got on the line. You came over and wanted to take the phone away from me. "Sure. Why don't you talk to Dr. Cotter," I said.

"Suzanne?"

"Yeah, I'm here, Connie. Taking it easy at home."

"Listen . . . we got your most recent bloods back. . . ."

Oh, that awful doctor's pause, that search for just the right wording. I know it only too well.

"And . . . I'm not happy. You're heading into the danger zone. I want to check you in right away. Start you on fluids. I'll show you the results on your bloods when you get here. How soon can that be?"

The words roared through my head with the force of a gale, taking all my strength with it. I was devastated. I had to sit down immediately. With the phone still to my ear, I lowered my head between my legs.

"I don't know, Connie. I'm here with Nicky. Matt's at work."

"Unacceptable, Suzanne. You could be in trouble, sweetie. I'll call Jean if you won't."

"No, no. I'll call her. I'll do it right now."

I hung up, and you held on to my hand like a strong little soldier. You knew just what to do — you must have learned it from your daddy.

I remember tucking you into your crib and pulling the cord on your music box. "Whistle a Happy Tune" begins to play. *It's so beautiful* — even in my nervous state of mind.

I remember turning on your night-light and closing the curtains.

I remember that I was on my way downstairs to call Grandma Jean, then Matt.

That's all I remember.

Matt found me lying as limp as a rag doll at the bottom of the stairs. I had a deep gash alongside my nose. Had I fallen down the entire flight? He called Grandma Jean and rushed me to the ER.

From there, I was transferred to the Critical Care Unit. I awoke to a whir of frantic activity around my bed. *Matt wasn't there anymore.*

I cried out for Matt, and both he and Connie were at my side in seconds. "You took a bad fall, Suzanne." Matt was the first to speak. "You passed out at the house."

"Is the baby okay? Connie, my baby?"

"We have a heart rate, Suzanne, but the situation isn't good. *Your* pressure is off the charts, your proteins are skyrocketing and . . ."

She paused long enough for me to know there was another big *and.*

"And what?" I asked.

"And you have toxemia. That could be

why you passed out at the house."

I knew what this abnormal condition meant, of course. My blood was poisoning both the baby and me. I had never heard of it occurring this early in a pregnancy, but Connie couldn't be wrong.

I was hearing what Connie was telling me in disjointed sound bites. I wasn't able to form whole sentences in my head. I felt as if I were being lobotomized. I thought I could actually feel the toxic blood swelling up inside me as if I were a dam about to break.

Then I heard Matt being ordered out of the room, and an emergency team rushing in. Doctors and nurses were swarming all around me. I could feel the oxygen mask covering my nose and my mouth.

I knew what was happening to me. In layman's terms:

My kidneys were shutting down.

My blood pressure was dropping.

My liver was barely functioning as guardian against the poisons.

My body was beginning to convulse.

Fluids and medications were given through an IV to stop the convulsions, but then I started hemorrhaging.

I knew I was shutting down. I knew so much more than I wanted to. I was scared. I was floating out of my body and then falling into a dark tunnel. The passing black walls were narrowing and squeezing the breath out of me.

I was dying.

Matt sits vigil by my bedside, day and night. Daddy never leaves me alone, and I worry about him. I have never loved him more than I do now. He is the best husband, the best friend, a girl ever had.

Connie visits constantly three or four times a day. I never knew what a great doctor she is, and what a great friend.

I hear her, and I hear Daddy. I just can't respond to either of them. I'm not sure why.

From what I can tell listening to them, I know that I've lost the baby. If I could cry, I would weep for all eternity. If I could scream, I would. I can do neither, so I mourn in the most awful silence imaginable. The sadness is bottled up inside and I ache to let it out.

Grandma Jean comes and sits with me for long stretches at a time, too. So do friends of mine from around the Vineyard, doctors from the hospital and even from Boston.

Melanie Bone and her husband, Bill, visit every day. Even Matt Wolfe, my lawyer friend, came by and whispered kind words to me.

I hear bits and pieces of what people are saying around me.

"If it's okay I'm going to bring Nicky in this afternoon," Daddy says to Connie. "He misses his mother. I think it's important he sees her." And then Matt says, "Even if it's for the last time. I think I should call Monsignor Dwyer."

Matt brings you to my hospital room, Nicholas. And then you and Daddy sit by my bedside all afternoon, telling me stories, holding my hand, saying good-bye.

I hear Matt's voice cracking, and I'm worried about him. A long time ago, his father died. He was only eight, and he never got over it. He won't even talk about his father. He's so afraid of losing someone again. And now it's me he's going to lose.

I just hold on. At least I think I'm still here. What other explanation can there be?

How could I possibly hear your laughter, Nicky? Or you calling out, "Mama," to me, in the black hole of my sleep?

But I do.

Your sweet little voice reaches down into my abyss and finds me in this deep dark place where I'm trapped. It is as if you and Daddy were calling me out of a strange dream, your voices like a beacon guiding me.

I struggle upward, reaching toward the sound of your voices — up, up, up.

I need to see you and Daddy one more time. . . .

I need to talk to you one more time. . . .

I feel a dark tunnel closing behind me, and I think that maybe I've found my way out of this lonely place. Everything is getting brighter. There is no more darkness surrounding me, just rays of warmth, and maybe the welcoming light of Martha's Vineyard.

Was I in heaven? Am I in heaven now? What is the explanation for what I'm feeling?

That's when the unexpected happens.

I *open* my eyes.

"Hello, Suzanne," Matt whispers. "Thank God, you came back to us."

Katie

There was only so much of the diary that Katie could take at any given time. Matt had warned her in his note: *there will be parts that may be hard for you to read.* Not just hard, Katie knew now, but overwhelming.

It was difficult for her to imagine right now, but there *were* happy endings in life.

There were normal, semisane couples like Lynn and Phil Brown, who lived in Westport, Connecticut, on a really cool little farm with their four kids, two dogs, and one rabbit and who were still in love as far as she or any of their other friends could tell.

The next day Katie called Lynn Brown and volunteered to sit for the kids that night, a one-night-only offer. She *needed* to be with the Browns. She needed the warmth and comfort of a family around her.

Lynn was immediately suspicious. "Katie, what's this all about? What's going on?"

"Nothing, I just miss you guys. Consider

it a pre-anniversary present for you and Phil. Don't look a gift horse in the mouth. I'm *in* Grand Central Station right now. I'm on my way."

She took the train to Westport and was at Lynn and Phil's by seven. At least she hadn't stayed late working at the office.

The Brown kids — Ashby, Tory, Kelsey, and Roscoe — were eight, five, three, and one. They loved Katie, thought she was so neat. They loved her long braid. And they loved that she was so *tall*.

So off went Lynn and Phil on their hot "date," and Katie took the kids. Actually, she was incredibly grateful to Lynn and Phil for "taking her in." They had met and liked Matt Harrison, and basically they knew what had happened between him and Katie. They didn't understand any of it, either. Lynn had predicted that Katie and Matt would be married within the year.

What a great night it turned out to be. The Browns had a small guest house that Phil was always threatening to fix up and make respectable. That was where Katie always went to hang out with the four kids.

They loved to play tricks on her, like hiding her suitcase and clothes or taking her makeup and putting it on (Roscoe included). She took the kids' pictures with her

Canon camera. They washed Lynn's Lexus SUV. Went on a group bike ride. Watched the movie *Chicken Run*. Ate an "everything" pizza.

When Lynn and Phil got home about eleven, they found Katie and the kids asleep on pillows and quilts thrown all over the guest-house floor.

She was actually awake and heard Lynn whisper to Phil, "She's so cool. She'll be a great mom." It brought tears to Katie's eyes, and she had to choke back a sob as she pretended to be asleep.

She stayed at the Brown house through Saturday afternoon. She finally took the six o'clock train back to New York. Before she left, she told Lynn that she was pregnant. She was exhausted, but she also felt alive again, rejuvenated — better, anyway. She believed in small miracles. She had hope. She knew there were some happy endings in life. She believed in families.

About halfway into the trip, Katie reached down into her bag and pulled out the diary.

She got off the train from Westport at the gorgeously renovated and restored Grand Central Station, and she needed to walk some. It was a little past seven-thirty and Manhattan was filled with traffic, most of it honking taxis or cars returning from weekend and vacation homes, the drivers *already* on edge.

She was on edge, too. The diary was doing that to her more and more.

She still didn't have the answer she needed to move on with her life. She wasn't over Matt — and she wasn't over Suzanne and Nicholas.

She was thinking about something she'd read earlier in the diary, the lesson of the five balls: work, family, health, friends, and integrity.

Work was a rubber ball, right?

Suzanne had figured that out, and her life had suddenly become peaceful and manageable. She had gotten away from all of *this:*

work, stress, pressure, deadlines, crowds pushing and shoving, road rage, life rage.

Immersing herself in someone else's reality had made Katie reexamine things that she had been doing on autopilot for the past nine years. She'd gotten her job at twenty-two, fresh out of the honors program at the University of North Carolina at Chapel Hill. She had been lucky enough to intern for two summers at Algonquin Press in Chapel Hill, which had opened important doors for her in Manhattan. So she had settled into New York City with the best of intentions, and loved so many things about it; yet she never felt that she truly fit, that New York City was where she was meant to be.

She still felt like a visitor here at times — a tall, gawky tourist.

Now she thought that maybe she knew why. Her life had been out of balance for such a long time. She had spent so many late nights at work or at home, reading and editing manuscripts, trying to make them as good as they could be. Rewarding work, but *work was a rubber ball, right?*

Family health, friends, and integrity were the precious glass ones.

The baby she was carrying was a glass ball for sure.

The following morning at about eleven, she was in a yellow cab with two of her best friends, Susan Kingsolver and Laurie Raleigh. She was going to see her gynecologist, Dr. Albert K. Sassoon, in the East Seventies.

Susan and Laurie were there for moral support. They knew about the pregnancy and had insisted on coming along. Each of them held one of Katie's hands.

"You feel okay, sweetie?" Susan asked. She was a grade-school teacher on the Lower East Side. They had met the one summer Katie had gone in on a summer house in the Hamptons, and had been best buddies ever since. Katie had been maid of honor at Susan's wedding, then a bridesmaid at Laurie's.

"I'm okay. Sure. I just can't make myself believe what's happened in the past few days. I can't believe I'm going to see Sassoon right now." *Oh, God, please help me. Please give me strength.*

As she got out of the taxi, Katie found that

she was blankly staring at pedestrians and familiar storefronts on East Seventy-eighth Street. What was she going to say to Dr. Sassoon? When Katie had been there for her yearly checkup, Albert was so incredibly excited to hear that she'd *found* someone — and now *this*.

Everything was a blur, even though Susan and Laurie were chatting amiably, keeping her *up*, doing a great job, really.

"Whatever you decide," Laurie whispered as Katie was called into Dr. Sassoon's examination room, "it will work out great. *You're* great."

Whatever she decided.

God, she just couldn't believe this was happening.

Albert Sassoon was smiling, and that made Katie think of Suzanne and her kindly way with patients.

"So," Dr. Sassoon said as Katie lay down and fitted her feet into the stirrups. Usually, Albert asked Katie not to hit him in the head with her knees. A little joke to lighten the moment. Not today, though.

"So. I was so much in love I stopped using my birth control. I guess I got knocked up," Katie said, and laughed. Then she was crying, and Albert came to her and tenderly held her head against his chest. "It's all right, Katie. It's all right. It's all right."

"I think I know what I'm going to do," Katie finally managed to say between sobs. "I think . . . I'm going . . . to keep . . . my baby."

"That's great, Katie," Dr. Sassoon said, and patted her back gently. "You'll be a wonderful mother. You'll have a beautiful child."

The Diary

Nicholas,

Today I came home from the hospital, and it's so unbelievably good to be here. Oh, I'm the luckiest girl in the world.

The familiarity of the rooms, your perfect nursery, the way the morning light comes spilling over the windowsills and lights all the things in its path. What a thrill to be here again. To be anywhere, actually.

Life is such a miracle, a series of small miracles. It really is, if you learn how to look at it with the right perspective.

I love our little cottage on Beach Road. More than ever, Nicky. I appreciate it more, every little crevice and crease.

Matt made a beautiful lunch for us. He's a pretty good cook — as handy with a spatula and skillet as he is with a hammer and nail. He laid out a picnic in the sunroom on a red-and-white-checkered blanket. A salad niçoise, fresh, twelve-grain bread, sun tea. Fabulous. After lunch the three of us sat there, and he held my hand and I held yours.

Nicholas, Suzanne, and Matt.

Happiness is this simple.

Nick, you little scamp,

Every moment with you fills me with such incredible wonder and happiness.

I took you into the Atlantic Ocean for the first time yesterday. It was the first day of July. You absolutely loved it.

The water was beautiful, with very small waves. Just your size. Even better was all the sand, your own private sandbox.

Big smiles from you.

And from me, of course.

Mommy see, Mommy do!

When we got home, I happened to show you a picture of two-year-old Bailey Mae Bone, our neighbor just down Beach Road. You started to smile, and then you *puckered* your lips. You're going to be a killer with the ladies. Be gentle, though, like your daddy.

You have good taste — for a guy. You love to look at pretty things — trees, the ocean, light sources, of course.

You also like to tickle the ivories on our piano, which is so cute.

And you love to *clean*. You push around a toy vacuum cleaner and wipe up messes with paper towels. Maybe I can take advantage of that when you're a little older.

Anyway, you are such a joy.

I treasure and hold close to my heart every giggle, every laugh, every needy cry.

"Wake up, beautiful. I love you even more today than I did yesterday."

Matt wakes me this same way every morning since I got home from the hospital. Even if I'm still half asleep, I don't mind being awakened by his soothing voice and those words.

The weeks passed, and I was getting my strength back. I began taking long walks on the beach in front of the cottage. I even saw a few patients. I exercised more than I ever had in my whole life.

A few more weeks passed, and I was even stronger. I was proud of myself, actually.

Matt was hovering over my bed again one morning. He was holding you, and smiling down on me. You both were grinning. I smelled a conspiracy.

"It's official! The three-day-long Harrison family weekend has begun. Wake up, beautiful. I love you! We're already late for today, though!"

"What?" I said, looking out the bedroom window. It was still dark outside.

You finally looked at your father as if he had gone completely bonkers.

"Down, *pup*," Matt said, putting you on my bed, beside me.

"Pack your bags. We're going away. Take whatever you need for three glorious days, Suzanne."

I was leaning on one elbow, staring curiously at Matt. "Three glorious days where?"

"I booked us into the Hob Knob Inn in Edgartown. King-size beds; full country breakfast, and afternoon tea. You won't have to lift a finger, wash a dish, or answer a telephone, Suzanne. Sound good?"

It sounded wonderful, exactly what I needed.

This is a love story, Nicholas. *Mine, yours, Daddy's!* It's about how good it can be if you find the right person. It's about treasuring every moment with that special one. *Every single millisecond.*

Our three-day adventure began at the Flying Horses Carousel, where we mounted the enchanted horses and circled the high hills of Oak Bluffs. There we were, riding the painted ponies under the bright umbrella, just like old times. What a rush!

We visited the beaches that we had been away from for so long. Lucy Vincent Beach off South Road, Quansoo and Hancock Beaches . . . private beaches that Matt, somehow, was able to get a key to gain entry.

We walked hand in hand in hand along Lighthouse Beach and Lobsterville Beach — and my very favorite, Bend in the Road Beach.

How invigorating it was to see those beaches again with Daddy and you. I can still see them now, and I can even see the three of us.

We took a carriage ride at Scrubby Neck Farm, and you couldn't stop laughing. You fed carrots to the horses, and you laughed so hard that I was afraid you might get sick. You glowed under the manes of the magnificent Belgian giants.

We ate at all the nicest restaurants, too. The Red Cat, the Sweet life Café, L'Etoile.

You looked like such a big boy in your high chair, sitting with us, so grown up, smiling in the candlelight.

We saw *Rumpelstiltskin* at the Tisbury Amphitheater and went to storytelling night at the Vineyard Playhouse. You were such a good boy at the *theater*.

Not far from where we were staying, there was a craft store called Splatter. We made our own cups and saucers.

You painted your plate, Nickels, drawing little splotches we took to be me and Daddy and yourself, in bright blues and soft yellows.

And then it was time to go home.

Nicky,

Do you remember any of this?

I noticed cars parked helter-skelter all along the side of Beach Road as we turned the last curve to our house. Several more cars, SUVs, and trucks were leading up to the driveway, but the strange thing was that *the driveway was no longer there.*

Instead, a new addition covered its place, and a new driveway lay on the far side of the addition, just as your daddy had promised.

"What," I asked Matt, shocked, "is all this?"

"A little extension, Suzanne. At least the humble beginnings of one. It's your new home office, and it has everything your old office didn't have. Now you can make less house calls, or *no* house calls. It's all right here in our backyard. Your office even has an ocean view."

Dozens of our friends and Matt's worker pals were on the lawn, applauding as we

257

climbed out of the car. You started to clap your hands, too, Nicky. I think you were clapping for yourself, though.

"Suzanne! Matt!" our friends were chanting in sync with the clapping. I was in awe, speechless, struck dumb. For three days Malt's coworkers and friends must have hammered day and night to create this unbelievable space.

"I still have to do the electrical work and plumbing," Matt said in an apologetic tone.

"This is too much," I said as I hugged him tight.

"No," he whispered back, "it isn't nearly enough, Suzanne. I'm just so happy to have you home."

Nicholas, sweet Nicholas,

Everything seems to be moving in the right direction again. The time is really flying. Tomorrow, you will be one! Isn't that something? *Dang!*

What can I say, except that it is a godsend to watch you grow up, to see your first tooth, watch you take your first step, say your first word, make a half sentence, develop your little personality day by day.

This morning you were playing with Daddy's big, bad work boots that he keeps at the bottom of the closet; when you came out, you were standing in them. You started to laugh; you must have thought this was the funniest joke anyone has ever played. Then I was laughing, and Daddy came in, and he started laughing, too.

Nicholas, Suzanne, and Matt! What a trio.

We're going to celebrate your first twelve months tomorrow. I have your gifts all picked out. One of them is the pictures from our vacation. I selected the best couple of shots, and I'm having them framed. I won't tell you which picture I like best; that'll be a surprise.

But I will tell you that it will be in a silver frame with carved moons and stars and angels all around it. Just your style.

It's almost time to sing "Happy Birthday!"

Nicholas,

It's late, and Daddy and I are being silly geese. It's a little past midnight, so it's *officially your birthday. Hoo-ray! Congratulations, you!*

We couldn't resist, so we sneaked into your room and watched over you for several moments. We held hands and blew you kisses. You know how to blow kisses, too. You're so smart.

Daddy brought along one of your birthday presents, a bright red Corvette convertible. He placed it carefully at the foot of your crib. You and your dad are both caraholics: you boys live for cars; you feel the need for speed.

Matthew and I hugged each other as we watched you sleep — which is one of the greatest pleasures in the world — *don't miss watching your child sleep.*

Then I got a little playful, and I pulled the cord on your music box. It played that

261

simple, beautiful song "Whistle a Happy Tune," which I know I will always associate with you sleeping in your crib.

Matt and I held each other and swayed to the music. I think we could have stayed there all night. Holding each other, watching you sleep, dancing to your music-box tune.

You didn't wake up, but a little smile crossed your face.

"Isn't it lucky?" I whispered to Matt. "Isn't this the best thing that could ever happen to anyone?"

"It is, Suzanne. It's so simple, but it's so right."

Finally, Daddy and I went to bed, and experienced the second best thing. Matt eventually fell asleep in my arms — guys do that if they really like you; and I got up to write this little note to you.

Love you, sweetie. See you in the morning. I can't wait.

Matthew

Hello, my sweet Nicholas, it's Dada.

Have I told you how much I love you? Have I told you how precious you are to me? There — *now I have*. You are the best little boy, the best anyone could ever hope for. I love you so much.

Yesterday morning something happened. And that's why I'm writing to you today instead of Mommy.

I am compelled to write this. I don't know anything for sure right now, except that I have to get this out. I have to talk to you.

Fathers and sons need to talk more than they do. A lot of us are so afraid to show our emotions, but I never want us to be like that. I always want to be able to tell you what I'm feeling.

Like right now.

But this is so hard, Nicky.

It's the hardest thing I have ever had to say to anybody.

Mommy was going to the store to pick up your birthday present, your beautiful framed pictures. She was incredibly happy. She looked so pretty, deeply tanned and toned from all her walks on the beach. I remember seeing her leave, and I can't get that image out of my mind.

Suzanne had such a beautiful smile on her face. She was dressed in a yellow jumper and gauzy white blouse. Her blond hair was full of curls and swung with her body as she walked. She was humming *your* song, "Whistle a Happy Tune."

I should have gone to her, should have kissed Suzanne good-bye, should have hugged her in my arms. But I just called, *"Love you,"* and since her hands were full, she blew me a kiss.

I keep seeing Suzanne blowing me that kiss. I see her walking away, looking back, giving me her famous wink. Imagining that playful wink of hers makes me tear up as I try to write this.

Oh, Nicky, Nicky, Nicky. How can I say this? How can I write these words?

Mommy had a heart attack on the way into town, sweet baby. Her heart, which was so big, so special in so many ways, could no longer hold out.

I can't imagine that it really happened; I

266

can't get it into my head. I was told that Suzanne was unconscious before she crashed into the guardrail on Old Pond Bridge Road. Her Jeep dropped into the water, landing on its side. I haven't gone to look at the actual scene of the accident. That is an image I don't need inside my head. What I can see already is too much.

Dr. Cotter says that Suzanne died instantly after the massive coronary, but who really knows about those final seconds? I hope she didn't feel any pain. I hate to think that she did. It would be too cruel.

She was unimaginably happy the last time I saw her. She looked so pretty, Nick. Oh God, I just want to see Suzanne one more time. Is that too much to ask? Is it unreasonable? It doesn't seem so to me.

It's important to me that you know it wasn't Mommy's fault. She was such a safe driver; she would never have taken any chances. I always teased her about her driving.

I loved Suzanne so much, and I can't begin to explain how lucky it is to find someone you can love that much and who, miracle of miracles, loves you that much back.

She was the most generous-hearted person I have ever known, the most caring and compassionate. Maybe what I loved best about her was that she was a great, great listener. And she was funny. She would make a joke, right now. I know she would. And maybe she is. *Are you smiling now, Suzanne?* I'd like to think that you are. I believe you must be.

I went today to the cemetery on Abel's Hill, to choose Mommy's special place. She was just thirty-seven when she died. How sad, how completely unthinkable to me, and everyone else who knew her. What a shame; what a waste. Sometimes it makes me so angry — and I get this strange, irrational urge to *break glass.* I don't know where it comes from, but I want to break glass!

Tonight I sit in your nursery and watch your clown lamp throw happy shadows against the walls in the half-light. The oak rocking horse I made for you reminds me of the Flying Horses Carousel. Remember when we all went there on our vacation and rode the colorful horses? *Nicholas, Suzanne, and Matt.*

I held you in front of me, and you loved to stroke the real horsehair mane. I can see Mommy riding ahead of us on National Velvet. She turns — and there's that famous wink of hers.

Oh, Nick, I wish I could turn back time to last week, or last month, or last year. I almost can't bear to face tomorrow.

I wish this had a happy ending.

I wish I could say just one more time: *Isn't it lucky?*

Dear sweet Nick,

There is one image that keeps coming back to me about Suzanne. It captures who she was, and what was so special and unique about her.

She is kneeling on our front porch one night. She wants my forgiveness, even though there is nothing to forgive. If anything, I should have been seeking her forgiveness. She had gotten some sad news that day but, in the end, could only think about how she might have hurt me. Suzanne always thought about other people first, but especially about the two of us. God, did she spoil us, Nicholas.

I was startled out of my thoughts and reveries this afternoon by an unexpected phone call.

It was for Mommy.

Obviously someone had no idea what had happened, and for the first time, those strange and awful words passed through my lips like heavy weights: "Suzanne has passed away."

There was a long silence on the other end, followed by quiet apologies, and then nervous condolences. It was the man from the frame shop on the other side of the island, in Chilmark Center. Mommy had never made it there, and the pictures she had framed for you were still at the store.

I told the shop owner that I would come around for the photos. Somehow, I would manage to do it. I feel so out of it all the time. I have a hollow feeling inside me, and it seems I could crumble like old tissue paper and blow away. At other times, there is a stone column inside my chest.

I never used to be able to cry, but now I cry all the time. I keep thinking that I'll run out of tears, but I don't. I used to think it wasn't manly to cry, but now I know that isn't so.

I walk aimlessly from room to room, trying desperately to find a place where I can feel at peace with myself. Somehow, I always end up back in your room, sitting in the same rocker Mommy so often did when she talked to you and read to you and recited her goofy rhymes.

And so I sit here now, looking at the pictures of us I finally picked up this afternoon in Chilmark.

We are all sitting in front of the Flying Horses Carousel on a perfect, blue-skied afternoon.

You are wedged between us, Nick. Mommy has her arm around you and her legs crossed on mine. You're kissing Mommy, and I'm tickling you, and everyone is laughing, and it's just so beautiful.

Nicholas, Suzanne, and Matt — Forever One.

It's time to tell you a story, Nick. It's a story that I will share only with you. It's just between the two of us.

Man to man, my little buddy.

Actually, it is the saddest story that I've ever heard, certainly the saddest one I've ever told.

I'm finding it hard to breathe right now. I'm shaking like a leaf. I have goose bumps all over my skin.

Years ago, when I was just eight, my father died very suddenly while he was at work. We didn't expect it, so we never got to say good-bye. For years, my father's death has haunted me. I've been so afraid of losing someone like that again. I think it's why I didn't get married earlier, before I met Suzanne. I was afraid, Nicky. Big, strong Daddy was so terribly afraid he might lose someone he loved. That's a secret I never told anyone before I met your mother. And now, I've told it to you.

I pull the cord on your music box in your crib, and it begins to play "Whistle a Happy Tune." I love this song, Nicky. It makes me cry, but I don't care. I love your music and I want to hear it again.

I reach into the crib and I touch your sweet cheek.

I tousle your golden blond hair, always so soft and fragrant. I wish I had listened to Mommy and never cut it.

I do a nose to nose, gently touching my nose to yours. I do another nose to nose and you smile gloriously. One of your smiles is worth the universe to me. That's the truth.

I place an index finger in each of your small hands and let you squeeze. You're so strong, buddy.

I listen to your beautiful laugh, and it almost makes me laugh.

"Whistle a Happy Tune" continues to play.

Oh my dear, darling little boy. Oh, my darling baby.

The music plays, but you *aren't* in your crib.

I remember Mommy leaving on her errand that morning. I called out "I love you," and she blew me a kiss. Then she crinkled up her nose the way she does. You know what I mean. You know that look of hers. Then she gave me her "famous wink," and I can see it right now. I can see Suzanne.

Her arms were full, because she was carrying *you,* sweet baby. She wanted you to be the first to see the beautiful framed photographs. That's why she took you with her to town on your birthday morning.

Suzanne carried you outside and carefully strapped you in your car seat. You were in the Jeep with Mommy when she crashed on Old Pond Bridge Road. The two of you were together. I still can't bear to think about it.

I should've been there, Nicholas. I should've been there with you and Mommy! Maybe I could have helped; maybe I could have saved you somehow. At least I could have tried, and that would have meant everything to me.

Oh sweetness, I need to hear your laugh one more time. I ache to look into your bright blue eyes. To nuzzle your soft cheek next to mine.

Oh my dear little boy, my innocent little sweetheart, my baby son forever. I miss you so much, and it destroys me that you will never know how I feel, that you will never hear how much your daddy loves you. I miss you so much, *I miss you so much,* sweet baby. I always will.

But isn't it lucky that I knew you, held you

and loved you, for the twelve months before God took you away?

Isn't it lucky that I got to know you, sweet little boy, my darling, darling son?

Katie

Katie slowly raised her face toward the bathroom ceiling and shut her eyes as tight as she could. A soft moan rose from her throat. Tears squeezed under her eyelids and rolled down both cheeks. Her chest was heaving. She wrapped both arms around herself.

Merlin was in the doorway, whining, and Katie whispered, "It's okay, boy."

A column of pain rose inside her like a hot poker cutting into her lungs. *Oh God, why would you let something like that happen?*

Finally, Katie opened her eyes again. She could barely see through her tears. There was an envelope taped inside the diary, on the very last page.

It said, simply, *Katie.*

She wiped away her tears with both hands. She took a deep, calming breath. And another. The breaths didn't help much. She opened the plain white envelope that was addressed to her.

The letter inside was in Matt's handwriting. Her fingers trembled as she unfolded it. The tears started again as she began to read.

Katie, dear Katie,

Now you know what I haven't been able to tell you all these months. You know my secrets. I wanted to tell you, almost since the day that we met. I have been grieving for such a long time, and I couldn't be comforted. So I kept my past from you. You, of all people. There are words from a poem about the local fishing boats and their crews that have been carved into the bar of Docks Tavern on the Vineyard. The longed-for ships / Come empty home or founder on the deep / And eyes first lose their tears and then their sleep. *I saw the words one night at Docks, when I couldn't cry anymore, and couldn't sleep, and I was almost crushed by the awful truth in them.*

Matt

That was all that he wrote, but Katie needed more. She had to find Matt.

She had always been a fighter. She'd conquered her fears to come to New York by herself. She'd always had the courage to do what she had to do.

Katie took the shuttle to Boston first thing in the morning. At Logan Airport, she was met by a car service that would take her to Woods Hole and the ferry to Martha's Vineyard.

She entered the Steamship Authority terminal in Woods Hole, bought her ticket, and got on a two-decker ferry called the *Islander*.

She had to talk to Matt. It was wrong not to let him know everything. It was just plain wrong, and she couldn't live that way. Matt needed to know about the baby.

During the seven-mile, forty-five-minute ride, she thought of Suzanne, and *her* arrival on the Vineyard after she left Boston. She wondered if Suzanne had been on board the *Islander*, too. She remembered the last words Suzanne had written to Nicholas: *I can't wait to see you in the morning.*

Katie realized she hadn't brought a manuscript to read on the plane or the ferry. *Work
is a rubber ball,* she thought. *Yes, it is.*

God, look at what she would have missed
if she had brought along paperwork: the
rhythmic chop of the waves against the ancient ferry's bow, the picturesque island of
Martha's Vineyard getting closer and closer,
the queasiness in her stomach every time a
big wave splashed into the ship.

*Matt was a glass ball. He had been scuffed,
marked, damaged, but maybe he hadn't been
shattered. Or maybe he had been.*

The mystery would never be solved unless
she found him.

As the *Islander* got closer and closer to the
Vineyard, Katie couldn't take her eyes off
the old Oak Bluffs ferry terminal. It was a
gray clapboard building, a one-story struc-
ture that looked a hundred years old if it was
a day. She could see a beach on one side of
the terminal, and the small town of Oak
Bluffs on the other.

Her eyes searched the terminal building,
the beach, the town — looking for Matt.

She didn't see him anywhere.

The town buildings of Oak Bluffs were across the street from the ferry terminal. There were several odd-colored taxis parked out front. And, of course, Matt wasn't waiting there for her to appear. He didn't know she was coming, and even if he had, he might not have come.

Katie spotted Docks Tavern as she started toward the taxi stand. Her heart skipped a beat. This had to be a sign, no? Had to be something. She walked toward the bar instead of searching for a cab.

Was Matt in there? Probably not, but Docks was where he had read the lines carved into the bar, which he had included in his note in the diary.

It was dark inside, a little smoky, pleasant enough, though. A Bruce Springsteen song played from an old Wellington jukebox. About a dozen patrons were at the bar, and several people were seated in the weathered wooden booths on either side. Most of them looked up at her as she entered. She knew she was having a bad hair day, bad clothes day, bad life day.

"I come in peace," Katie said, and smiled.

She was incredibly nervous, though. She had decided she was coming to Martha's Vineyard about three in the morning. She had to see Matt again. She wanted to be in his arms and to hold him, even if that might not happen. Katie needed a hug badly.

Her eyes roamed slowly over the faces, which seemed right out of *The Perfect Storm*. Her heart sped up some. She didn't see Matt. Well, thank God, he wasn't a regular at least.

She went looking for the poem carved into the bar. It took her a few minutes to find it at the far end, near a dartboard and a public phone. She read the words again:

The longed-for ships.
Come empty home or founder on the deep.
And eyes first lose their tears and then their sleep.

"Help you with something? Or is your interest wholly literary?"

She looked up at the sound of the male voice. She saw a bartender, mid-thirties, red-bearded, ruggedly good-looking. Maybe a sailor himself.

"I'm just looking for someone. A friend. I think he comes in here," she said.

"He has good taste in taverns, anyway. Does he have a name?"

She took in a breath and tried to keep the tremor out of her voice. "Matt Harrison," Katie said.

The bartender nodded, but his dark brown eyes narrowed. "Matt comes in here for dinner sometimes. He paints houses on the island. You say you're a friend of his?"

"He also writes books," Katie said, feeling a little defensive now. "Poetry."

The bartender shrugged, and continued to look at her suspiciously. "Not that I know of. At any rate, Matt's not here today. As you can see for yourself." The red-bearded man finally smiled at her. "So what will it be? You look like a Diet Coke to me."

"No, nothing, thanks. Could you tell me how to get to his place? I'm a friend of his. I'm his editor. I have the address."

The bartender thought about it, and then he tore a sheet off his order pad. "You driving?" he asked as he began to write down a few directions.

"I'll probably take a cab."

"They'll know the place," the man said, but didn't elaborate. "Everybody knows Matt Harrison."

Katie slowly climbed into a rusted sky blue Dodge Polaris cab at the ferry terminal. Suddenly she was feeling tired. She said to the driver, "I'd like to go to the Abel's Hill Cemetery. Do you know it?"

By way of an answer, the cabdriver simply pulled away from the curb. She guessed he knew where everything was on the island. She certainly hadn't meant to offend him.

Abel's Hill was a good twenty minutes away, a small, picturesque place that looked at least as old and historic as any of the houses they had passed on the way there.

"I won't be too long," she said to the driver as she struggled out of the backseat. "Please wait for me."

"I'll wait, but I have to keep the meter running."

"That's fine. I understand," she told him, and shrugged. "I'm from New York City. I'm used to it."

The cab waited while she slowly and reverently walked from row to row in Abel's Hill, checking all the headstones, but especially the newer ones. During the ride over, the cabdriver had told her that John Belushi and the writer Lillian Hellman were buried here.

Her chest felt tight, and there was a lump in her throat as she searched for the grave. She felt as if she were intruding.

Finally she found it. She saw the carved lettering on a stone set on a hill, *Suzanne Bedford Harrison.*

Her heart clutched again, and she felt dizzy. She bent and went down on one knee.

"I had to come, Suzanne," she whispered. "I feel as if I know you so well by now. I'm Katie Wilkinson."

Her eyes traveled across the inscription. *Country doctor, much loved wife of Matthew, perfect mother of Nicholas.*

Katie offered up a prayer, one that her father had taught her when she was only three or four.

She turned to the smaller stone right beside Suzanne's. She sucked in a breath.

Nicholas Harrison, a real boy, cherished son of Suzanne and Matthew.

"Hello, sweet baby boy. Hello, Nicholas. My name is Katie."

She began to sob uncontrollably then.

She clutched her chest with both arms, and her whole body shook like a weeping willow in a storm. She mourned for poor baby Nicholas. She couldn't begin to understand how Matt had survived this.

She imagined him in Nicholas's room, playing the music box on the crib over and over, trying to remember how it had been with his baby son, trying to bring Nicholas back.

There were flowers, daisy poms, carnations, and gladiolas at both of the graves. *Someone has been here recently, maybe even today.* Matt had always given her roses. He was a good man, sweet and kind. She'd been right about that. She hadn't made a bad choice, just an unlucky one.

And then Katie noticed something else, the date that was carved into the two headstones.

July 18, 1999.

She felt a shiver vibrate through her, and her knees were weak again. July 18 was two years to the day of the party she'd had planned for Matt on her terrace in New York, the night she'd given him the copy of his book of poems. No wonder he ran away. And now, where was Matt?

Katie had to see him — one more time.

It took another twenty minutes for the creaky island cab to bump its way from the cemetery to the old boathouse that she immediately recognized as Suzanne's.

It was painted white now. The barnlike doors and the trim were gray. There was a flower garden full of hydrangeas, azaleas, and daylilies.

She could see why Suzanne had loved it so much. Katie did, too. It was a real home.

She slowly got out of the cab. An ocean breeze played with her hair. She felt the wind gently pat her face and her bare legs. Her heart was back into its pounding routine again.

"Should I wait?" the driver asked.

Katie nibbled her upper lip, crossed and uncrossed her long arms. She looked at her watch: 3:28. "No. Thanks. You can go this time. I'll be here for a while."

She paid the driver, and he sped off.

Her heart was stuck in her throat as she

walked up the gravel path to the house. Her eyes did a once-over of the property. She saw no sign of Matt. No car. Maybe it was in back.

She knocked on the front door, waited, fidgeted, then used the old wooden knocker.

No one answered.

God, it was so weird to be here.

Her heart just wouldn't stop pounding.

She didn't see a sign of anyone at the house, but she was determined to wait for Matt. She could almost imagine him showing up now: old jeans, a khaki shirt, work boots, welcoming smile.

Would Matt smile if he saw her here? She needed to talk to him, to get some things off her chest. It was her turn to talk. She deserved that much. She had secrets she needed to share.

So she waited and waited. Then Katie sat on the front lawn for a while, massaging her stomach gently, listening to the waves. Eventually she crossed Beach Road . . . where Suzanne's dog, Gus, had been struck by a speeding red truck.

She sat on the beach where Matt and Suzanne had danced in the moonlight. She could *see* them. And then she imagined dancing with Matt again. He wasn't a great dancer, but she had loved being in his strong arms. She didn't like admitting it now, but it was the truth. It would always be the truth.

She thought that she probably had most of the mystery solved: Matt couldn't get Suzanne and Nicholas out of his mind, couldn't stop grieving. He probably didn't think that he ever could. Maybe he couldn't bear the thought of losing someone again. He had lost his wife and year-old child, and even his father when he was just a boy.

She couldn't blame him; she really couldn't. Not since she'd read the diary and understood what he had been through. If anything, and this really hurt her, she loved Matt more now than she ever had.

Katie picked her head up and saw a small, dark-haired woman in a pale blue dress, but barefoot. She was walking toward her across Beach Road. Katie didn't take her eyes off her.

When the woman was close, she said, "You're Melanie Bone, aren't you?"

Melanie had the nicest, friendliest smile, just what she would have imagined. "And you're Katie. You're Matthew's editor from New York. He told me about you. He said you were willowy and pretty; that you usually wore your dark hair in a braid but sometimes loose strands fell across your cheeks."

Katie wanted so much to ask Melanie what else Matt had said, but she didn't, couldn't. "Do you know where he is?" she asked.

Melanie grimaced and shook her head. "He's not here. I'm sorry, Katie. I don't know where Matt is. We're all worried about him, actually. I was hoping that he was with you in New York."

"He's not," Katie said. "I haven't seen him, either."

Late in the afternoon Melanie gave Katie a ride back to the ferry terminal in Oak Bluffs. The kids rode in the back of the station wagon. They were just about as good-natured as their mother. They liked Katie right away and she liked them.

"Don't give up on him," Melanie said as Katie was about to walk away to board the *Islander*. "He's worth it. Matt's had the worst experience of anyone I know. But I think he'll recover. He's a really good person. Handy around the house, too. And Katie, I know he loves you."

Katie nodded, and she waved good-bye to the Bone family. Then she left Martha's Vineyard the way she had come there, alone.

Another long, bad week passed for her. Katie fell deeper and deeper into her work, but she thought a lot about going home to North Carolina. For good. She would have the baby there, among the people she loved and who loved her.

Katie hadn't been in the office very long that Monday morning when she heard her name being called.

She had just transferred her tea from the blue Le Croissant paper cup to the antique china one she kept on her desk. Her stomach didn't feel too bad that morning. Or maybe she was just getting used to it.

"Katie? Come over here right now. Katie! Now."

She was slightly annoyed. "What, *what?* I'm coming. Hold your horses."

Her assistant, Mary Jordan, was poised behind a floor-to-ceiling window that looked down on East Fifty-third Street. She motioned for Katie to come to the window.

"Come *here!*"

Curious, she walked to the window and looked down on the street. She spilled hot tea on herself, nearly dropping her antique cup, until Mary reached out and deftly snatched it from her.

Katie then walked past Mary, down the short hallway of the publishing-house offices, to the single elevator. Her knees were weak, her head spinning. She was self-consciously brushing strands of hair away from her face. She didn't know what to do with her hands.

She passed the publisher and owner, who was getting out of the elevator. "Katie, I need to talk —" He started to say something, but she cut him off with a raised hand and a shake of the head. "I'll be right back, Larry," she said, then rushed into the elevator, which was just starting back down. The publishing-house offices were on the top floor.

Time to compose yourself, she thought.

No, not enough time. Not even close.

The elevator descended to the first floor without making any stops.

Katie stood in the lobby and forced herself to be very still inside. Her thoughts were amazingly concise, actually. Suddenly everything seemed so clear and simple to her.

She thought about Suzanne, about Nicholas, and about Matt.

She thought about the lesson of the five balls.

Then Katie walked outside the building and onto the streets of New York. She took a deep breath as the warmth of the sunshine struck her face.

Dear God, make me strong enough for whatever is going to happen now.

She saw Matthew on Fifty-third Street.

He was kneeling on the sidewalk, less than a dozen feet away from where Katie stood, right in front of her office building. His head was bowed slightly. He was courteous and considerate enough to have placed himself out of the main pedestrian flow. She couldn't take her eyes off him.

Of course, *everyone* looked at him as they passed. How could they resist? Rubbernecking was an art in New York City.

He looked good: tan, trim, his hair a little longer than usual; jeans, a clean but frayed chambray shirt, dusty work boots. He looked like the Matt she knew, the Matt she had loved, and realized now that she still did.

Kneeling in front of her building. Right there in front of her.

Just as Suzanne had knelt that one night on their porch — to ask forgiveness, even though there was nothing to forgive.

Katie believed she knew what she had to

do. She followed her instincts on this, followed her heart.

She took a breath, then she got down on one knee beside Matt, facing him, very close to him, as close as she could get. Her heart was thundering. *Thump-thump, thump-thump.*

She had wanted to see Matt one more time, and here he was. Now what?

Pedestrians were starting to clog up the sidewalk. A few of them made unkind remarks, complaining about the loss of a few precious seconds on their journeys to work, or wherever it was that they rushed off to every morning.

Matt reached out his hand. Katie hesitated, but then she let him take her long, thin hands in his.

She had missed his touch. Oh God, she had missed this.

She had missed a lot about him, but especially the way she felt at peace when he was with her.

Strangely, she was starting to feel calm now. What did that mean? What was supposed to happen next?

Why was he here? To apologize or explain in person? What?

Finally Matt raised his head and looked at her. She had missed those soft brown eyes, even more than she thought. She'd missed his strong cheekbones, the furrowed brow, his perfect lips.

Matt spoke, and, God, she had missed the sound of his voice. "I love looking into your eyes, Katie, the honesty I see there. I love your country drawl. You're so unique, and I treasure that. I love being with you. I never tire of it. Not for one minute since I've known you. You are a great editor. You're a great carpenter, too. You *are* tall, but you *are* ravishing."

Katie found that she was smiling. She couldn't help it. Here they were, the two of them, on their knees in midtown. Nobody could possibly understand what they were doing and why. Maybe not even they themselves understood.

"Hello, stranger," she said. "I went looking for you, Matt. I traveled to the Vineyard. I finally got up there."

Matt smiled now. "So I heard. From Melanie and the kids. They thought you were ravishing, too."

"What else?" Katie asked. She needed to know more, to learn more, anything that he would tell her. God, she was so glad to see him again. She couldn't have imagined how glad she would be, how this would feel.

"What else? Well, the reason I'm here, on my knees, is I want to give myself over to you,

Katie. I'm sure of it. I'm finally ready. I'm yours, if you'll have me. I want to be with you. I want to have children with you. I love you. I'll never leave you again. I promise, Katie. I promise with all my heart."

And then, they finally kissed.

That October on the gorgeous Outer Banks of North Carolina, Katie Wilkinson and Matt Harrison were married at the Kitty Hawk Chapel.

The Wilkinson and Harrison families hit it off famously right from the start. The two families immediately became one. Katie's friends from New York all came down, spent a few extra days at the beach, and got lobster pink, of course. Her North Carolina friends preferred the cover of porches and shade trees. Both groups of friends reached agreement on the mint juleps.

Katie was thin, but she wasn't showing too much. Only a few of the wedding guests knew that she was going to have a baby. When she had told Matt, he hugged and kissed her and said he was the happiest, luckiest person in the world.

"Me, too," said Katie. "Actually, me three."

It was a simple but beautiful wedding and reception, held under cloudless blue skies with temperatures hovering in the low seventies. Katie looked like an angel, white, with wings. Tall. Ravishing. The wedding was completely unpretentious from beginning to end. The tables were decorated with family photographs. The bridesmaids carried pale pink hydrangeas.

While they were exchanging vows, Katie couldn't help thinking to herself, *Family, health, friends, integrity — the precious glass balls.*

She understood it now.

And that was how she would live the rest of her life, with Matt and their beautiful baby.

Isn't it lucky.